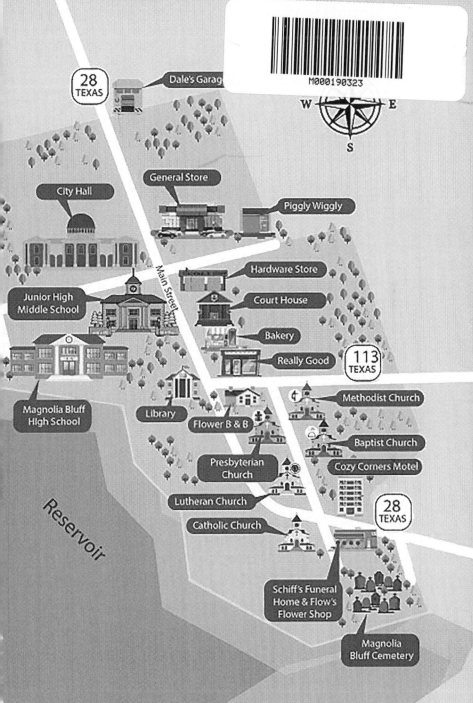

Magnolia Bluff

Time to Let it GO

JJ rocked back in his leather office chair, shaking his head as he scanned the latest email, then replied to the text in capital letters on his cell phone. Fingers of his left hand scrubbed back his thick black hair in response to the nonstop requests for support. He led the Cyber Assassin Technology Services or CATS team as the CTO. His business, based in São Paulo supported global customers with their end-to-end digital operations for telecommunications, networking, digital security, and physical security needs. He checked his watch as it slowly ticked down, and sighed. "I only have a few more items to complete until paradise," he mumbled to himself, then tackled the latest issues that crashed into his inbox.

His fingertips raced across the keyboard like a violin master playing "Flight of the Bumblebee" at London's Royal Albert Hall when he was interrupted by a call. "Hey, what's up?... You've moved new requests to your inbox…Cool. Let me finish this last note, and I'm outta here…Oh yay. I'm leaving for my getaway no matter what. You're in charge. No one gets time off without a great reason until I get back…That's right, I'm back in ten days…Thanks, man."

The final report nearly completed itself with a few enthusiastic keystrokes. After hitting send, JJ powered down his laptop and secured it, along with the power cable, into his worn leather backpack.

Feeling older than this twenty-five years, he stood and stretched beyond his normal six feet. His movements flexed his muscles maintained with daily workouts or sparring with his uncle. Absentmindedly, he finger-combed his hair and picked up his cell. Without looking in the mirror, JJ knew the grin on his face was there for the duration of the trip. He thumbed a message onto the screen with rapid-fire strokes.

> Jo, honey, I'm finished here. On my way to get you.

Seconds later the response appeared.

> I'm packed and ready. Heading to the front now.

Paul guided the limo to the driveway in time for JJ to see her hug goodbye to her adoptive parents and turn to him with a smile. Jo grabbed her bag, gave another quick wave from the bottom step, then danced down the steps in her short shorts that showed her bronzed legs. Her long sable brown hair was visible on either side of her trim waist.

Jo captured JJ's attention as much today as the day they'd met when his Aunt Lara decided to bring this lovely orphan to Brazil to work for Destiny Fashions. His breath quickened along with his pulse. Jo connected to his soul. With their long-distance careers, he hoped this trip would make their relationship more permanent. JJ timed it perfectly to open the passenger door with a flourish.

"Hi, JJ," she said with a grin, and, rising to her tiptoes, gave him a quick hug.

He offered a hand to help her into the car then turned to wave at his aunt and uncle. "I'll bring her back safe and sound."

The trunk opened and he added her bag, then made his

way to the other passenger door, climbed in, and fastened his seatbelt. "Paul, please head to the airport."

JJ pulled her close to him with his right arm and looked into her chocolaty brown eyes, bright with anticipation. "Are you ready for our adventure, my sweet? I'll pick our rental car up in Austin."

Jo's smile radiated her face, and her gentle hand smoothed his cheek and neck. She whispered as she leaned into him, "Yes, honey. I'm looking forward to our time together."

"Aunt Petra told me about the beautiful wine country in Texas. I found us a quaint bed and breakfast in a small town in an area called the Hill Country. Hopefully no one will pester you for autographs. It's a small town in a remote country area, well away from the constant work demands we both have. Aunt Petra said that we can rent motorcycles to see the countryside."

Her eyes widened with excitement. "Motorcycles? Wow. I've never been on a bicycle, let alone a motorcycle. You drive, I ride. Horseback riding, I could handle."

"Hmm. The world's hottest teen model superstar can ride a horse. We'd better not let your fans know or they'll want you to endorse a Kentucky horse show or something."

Jo playfully swatted his thigh and laughed. "You are so funny. I'm not that famous. I'm just having fun wearing pretty clothes for Destiny Fashions."

CHAPTER ONE

Peace and Quiet

JJ sighed with relief when the GPS indicated the last turn to Flower B&B a mile up the gravel filled road.

"JJ." Jo pointed out the window. "Look at that church steeple. I bet there's a bell. You said the town wasn't too far from where we're staying, right?"

"Exactly. We're coming from outside of the main town. When I called, the owner said we could walk to the square, but to bring walking shoes. Did you?"

"Yes, and my swimsuit for the reservoir you mentioned if it's hot. I even bought a pair of cowboy boots so you can take me dancing."

Surprised, JJ swerved the car due to his slight distraction. "I don't know about the dancing part, but I'll try. I can't resist a chance to have you in my arms."

He parked in front of the quaint two-story clapboard building. Lace curtains swayed to the breeze from the open windows upstairs.

"Wow, JJ, this is so pretty. Bursts of purple, white, and yellow blooms are all around this place. The name makes sense now. The grey with white trim creates the perfect canvas for these flowers." She leaned over and kissed his cheek. "This is a fabulous place."

Not as amazing as you, he thought.

She opened the door and climbed from the car, out of habit adding her sun hat and dark glasses at the last minute.

He extracted the bags from the trunk and handed Jo hers. His arm settled around her waist and tugged her close. "It's better than the website's photos. What an ordeal to get here though. They need a map for visitors. My GPS had trouble finding Magnolia Bluff as well as Flower B&B."

Giggling, Jo added, "I liked when you tried to explain to the people you asked where we were going, and they felt you were nuts to go to a B&B in such a little town. I don't understand why there were so many California license plates in Austin, Texas. California must have really ticked off their citizens. Still, thank you for finding this gem. The traffic is easier to maneuver than São Paulo."

"You've got that right, babe. Come on. Let's check in and chill for the rest of the afternoon. Perhaps a little white wine for you and a quart of tequila for me might take the edge off."

"You're so funny. You don't like tequila. I'm looking forward to a warm, soapy bubble bath in that clawfoot tub you saw in the photos."

"Small towns have a way of unwinding people with their laid-back pace of life."

They held hands, and the sounds of voices increased as they walked around the corner. It surprised them to see a small crowd gathered at the entrance.

JJ whispered into her ear, inhaling her delightful fragrance. "These folks must love the food Flower serves; the reviews were great."

"What's up?" Jo asked a woman in a flowered-print shirt, jeans, and a cowboy hat. "We didn't expect a crowd."

The woman smiled and offered, "A group of ladies are doing a special podcast today. Everyone likes to show up and listen to the latest community issue, or even heckle, if given a chance." The woman turned searching the faces on the porch. "Hey, Lily. You've got guests stuck on the wrong side of the pod-crowd."

An elderly woman with glasses covering bright blue eyes, her face framed by jet-black hair, held up a waving hand and bellowed, "Kids. Over here, and don't mind the gawkers. They just want a chance to hear the fresh gossip. Come on, everyone, make like the Red Sea and part so Moses can get through! Don't fret about missing something on the podcast 'cause it ain't started yet!"

Lily pulled JJ along in close tow. Jo right behind him giggled as Lily observed, "You're a handsome thing." Once inside, Lily became all business. "Juan Rodreguiz and his lady JoAnn Wagner, correct? You didn't say married but never you mind, I'm not some prude who doesn't understand what some people do to be together. And no, I won't send a thank you card to your address that might be read by the real Mrs. Rodreguiz. I've only made that mistake once." Barely taking a breath she continued, "Sorry about the podcast crowd. Our leader, Mary Lou Fight used to head up the Crimson Hat Society, but it disbanded some time ago. She was injured and is doing therapy to get out of that chair permanently. Our Pod-Team goes from business to business for important issues like this Mateo Hernandez character. He erected an eight-foot wall around his recently acquired ranch. The secrecy makes this a popular topic so small businesses in town fought for the right to host the broadcast from their shop for the advertising. Ever since my husband passed away, I've been trying to make this B&B earn its keep. Mr. Rodreguiz, you didn't say much about your line of work or Miss JoAnn's. You're not wanted by the authorities, are you?"

Surprised at the pause, JJ was impressed by the woman's non-stop conversation and noted the skepticism in her question. "Please, call me JJ. As I said when I made the reservation, we're looking for some quiet time. We're not married, but we love one another. I've no wife in hiding. I do work in customized security. We've had a long trip. We'd like to check in and enjoy your lovely establishment."

Undaunted, Lily leaned close to JoAnn. "I get it, sweetie. He wants to marry you but hasn't asked yet. You're pretty, so he's likely scared you'd turn him down. He's a hunk. You look like a nice couple. Don't fret about him getting away. Do you need beverages or snacks to take up? I can provide wine and beer if you'd rather."

JJ loved the rosy glow growing on Jo's cheeks as she seemed enthralled with their innkeeper. This black-haired fireball knew all about the U.S. filibuster process. Cute, independent, and feisty.

Lily reached her hand out with the key and room number when the podcast team in the dining area exploded with multiple shrieks of anguish. Lily pushed their room key into JJ's hand and clutched her hand to her heart as a podcaster cried, "No! No! No! This can't be happening! Not now, dammit!"

Lily rushed around the counter and faced the four women as JJ watched. "What's wrong, Mary Lou? You're almost ready to start, aren't ya? The listeners are counting on our queen bee of community information for the straight scoop today."

Mary Lou straightened up and bellowed, "Our computer equipment's poisoned. Look at this ugly note on the screen demanding Bitcoin tokens to unlock our equipment. If my computer won't work, there's no podcast today."

Lily strode into the room and bent down nose-to-nose with Mary Lou. "No, you can't! I need the advertising boost for my business. I have my latest B&B meal deals to share with the listeners. Don't give up. You can fix it."

JJ started toward the stairs holding Jo's hand—when she stopped. "JJ, you might be able to help. It's okay if you try. We'll have fun when it's fixed, and you won't pace about it in our room."

He looked up the stairs, shook his head, then started toward the group of older women. "Lily," he said as he walked toward the group. "I might be able to do something, I'm good with computers. Miss Mary Lou, may I please take a look?"

Mary Lou eyed him from head to toe, making him feel like he was being undressed, and not by the right female. Smiling and adding a sassy flirt, she purred, "Why, certainly, young man. You call me Mary Lou. Make this machine work and there'll be hugs and kisses."

Suppressing a cringe at that imagery, he walked over to the machine and sat to analyze the situation. "Jo, can you bring me my laptop, please?" He felt the five pairs of eyes drilling into his brain but didn't let the discomfort show.

"Here, JJ. Let me know if you need anything else." She plucked the key from his hand, and added, "I'm going to run our bags up to our room and be right back."

He used his machine to discover more about the problem as he rebooted Mary Lou's system. The speed of his fingers over the keyboard and associated clicking blanked out the noise around him. "Mary Lou, can you please write down your username and password for me?"

Mary Lou scribbled the information on her notepad.

JJ nodded his thanks with a short grin and returned to the keyboard. Ten minutes passed, and the machine presented its normal screen.

Cheers erupted from Mary Lou, followed closely behind by her friends.

"Girls, I don't know what this young man did, but we're gonna have our show. Lily, freshen up your hair and lipstick. We're going live in five."

JJ cleared his throat for attention. "Ladies, the ransomware message on your devices came from an illegal gambling site that specializes in hurting visitors who look but don't spend. The browser cookies suggest these machines visited sites with adult content. In my experience, web surfing to unknown sites is ill-advised."

Lily, in total disbelief, slowly rotated her gaze to the podcast team. Stomping her feet and seething, she announced, "Mary Lou Fight, Caroline McCluskey, Valerie Rheinhart, we'll hold that discussion 'til later. Stop looking away from me. Let's start the podcast."

JJ grinned. "Miss Lily, I'll take you up on a bottle of chilled wine if you have one, please. I understand Texas wines are quite delicious."

The podcast team scrambled to complete their setup as Lily smiled at her newest guest. "I will if you call me Lily."

CHAPTER TWO

Romantic Undertones

JJ grabbed his laptop and clasped Jo's hand, guiding her toward the stairs. He led her up the red rose carpeted stairs looking for their door. He planned a relaxing afternoon with the woman of his dreams.

Jo paused and commented on the various framed flower pictures that decorated the ivory walls. "JJ, wait. Look at this blue field of flowers. The title says, Texas Bluebonnets. I've never seen a prettier sea of blossoms."

Encircling her with his arms from behind, JJ added a hug as he inhaled her fresh scent. "I don't know, honey. The color reminds me of the first dress you wore for Aunt Lara in the dress shop she was visiting to promote her creations. One look and you convinced her to hire, then later adopt you." He recalled how captivating she was in the simple outfit. "The skirt of that dress floated around you like wings."

"You're so sweet. I wore that dress often. Let's go to our room so I can properly thank you for remembering. It's the last door."

He grinned at this sweet young woman he was delighted to have to himself for a few days. He opened the door into an inviting hideaway and pulled her inside.

"JJ, this is lovely and peaceful with the pale green walls. The lovely bedding of green leaves on a white background goes well with the lace curtains."

JJ connected his cell Bluetooth to the speaker on the night-stand allowing their favorite smooth jazz to float on the air in the background. "Soothing I think is a great word, and not just girly." He opened the attached door. "Honey, look at this. An original footed tub so you can have that bubble bath. I am so happy to scrub your back anytime you wish."

She squealed with delight, adding a kiss on his cheek. "Thank you for finding this place. It's simple but very enchanting."

They opened their bags to unpack. Season travelers, they quickly picked drawers and hangers for their belongings. JJ finished first. He stood staring out the window, appreciating the blue skies and flower-shaped shadows on the ground that came to life as sunshine fell upon the pedals. Distracted, he randomly combed his hair with his fingers. "I can hear them through the floor setting up for the podcast, based on the orders by that Mary Lou character. Her voice would be useful to warn ships off the rocky coast of Nova Scotia when the fog hits. I'm only hearing part of the discussion, but it sounds like things are getting ready to go."

"Did you want to go watch or listen?"

"Not necessarily. There is something that doesn't make sense. The links to those questionable sites I mentioned to the group didn't show any clicks or downloads. I tend to question oddness when it makes no sense. They all struck as nice ladies. I hope no one is setting them up."

Jo stepped up and wound her fingers into his hand. He liked the feel of her warmth. He kissed her sweet lips but was still distracted.

"JJ, I bet you want to go check it out. Let's go listen. I've never watched a live podcast as a spectator. It'll be a learning experience."

JJ looked deep into her sparkling eyes. "How is it that you're so agreeable? I'm here to work on our relationship and charm you, not threats from some digital monster. You're here to escape the centerstage for a bit. I promised no one would bother us here, but you want to go watch the circus?"

"You did say we could do anything we wanted."

JJ laughed. "Got me there. Let's go watch the locals do their hometown podcast about the community. Heck, we'll find out about farming, upcoming fundraisers, and kids in 4H."

Jo hip-bumped him. "JJ, be nice. You're distracted by an unsolved puzzle, and I want to watch."

JJ kissed her again. "Come on, let's go watch and heckle if we get a chance. Maybe there's popcorn."

CHAPTER THREE

The Podcast Must Go On

Lily started to relax when Mary Lou settled into the center chair. From her position she watched everything inside. Mary Lou's husband, Gunter, was on outside duty with the folks who wanted to be at the live event and maybe ask questions that would be aired. He wouldn't stick around when the show ended unless Mary Lou told him to stay.

As the former leader of the Crimson Hat Society, now head of the community podcasters, Mary Lou sat perfectly still with shoulders back, chest up. She patted her styled, grayish hair gently, knowing nothing was amiss, and smiled as she fired orders to her team. "Valerie, you're in this segment with me, so git over here and sit. LouEllen, move that light up a little but make certain not to add wrinkle shadows. We're live in four minutes. Caroline, you're doing the live questions if they call in on the meeting line. Lily, let the watch-party know. Remind them no shout-outs unless I say so."

Lily scampered to the front door, opened it, and delivered her message. She returned to her catbird seat and saw the signal from Mary Lou. She sat at the operations set-up and cued the introduction video. She murmured, "I'm so glad I asked Father Gorman to do the voice-over for our intro. His voice is like fine whiskey—smooth and warm. He's the reason more folks attended Christ of the King on Sundays."

The music dissolved into the background, and the collective sigh from the ladies punctuated the warm baritone voice of Lee Gorman. "Ladies and gentlemen, thank you for joining the podcast. During today's discussion, Mary Lou may open it up for questions and comments. Our sponsor of this show is Lily Greenly, owner of Flower Bed and Breakfast. Lily is offering a special this week: buy two breakfasts and get a free lunch any time this month, during work hours, of course. Now here's What's Happening in Magnolia Bluff."

Mary Lou started, "Good afternoon, friends, followers, and neighbors. My, um…our podcast spotlights events in and around Magnolia Bluff. Our latest promotion plan features our show at various businesses every other day. This is show number four today. Joining me are Valerie and LouEllen for our discussion.

"Ladies, let me ask a question to start us off. Why do you think people like Mateo Hernandez come into our community, buy up property, then don't introduce themselves? The county records show Superior Import and Export, represented by Wiley E. Purloin of the Cheatham, Pilferus, and Pocketum Law Firm. The good people of this community need to know who is moving into our community and why, but we're not getting any of that. Ladies, help me out here."

Valerie piped up. "We're on these unsociable people coming into our community. They're strange. Mr. Hernandez keeps his distance and uses outside contractors to work on his property. Has anyone in these parts ever erected a privacy screen eight feet high, and posted a rent-a-cop at the gate before starting construction? With all the immigrants pushing through the border illegally, I even went as far as making inquiries with a government contact to see if this is part of a Homeland Security initiative."

Mary Lou's eyes widened. "Oh my! I hadn't thought of that! What did they say, Valerie?"

"After they stopped laughing, they told me to mind my own business."

LouEllen giggled then cleared her throat. "Didn't you tell them we're on a mission to unearth material for our community? Our podcast is designed to dig for the truth no matter how many folks get upset. You should have broken into the lyrics from that famous Lonnie Lupnerder tune:

♫   *We Be Reporting on the various sundries!*   ♫
People's love your dirty undies!

Mary Lou regained control. "Ladies, y'all know that in this country, folks have a right to their privacy even if it does rankle us. Codswallop. We'll open a Freedom of Information request and demand answers for strange goings on. We might try the same with old Wiley E. Purloin. He needs to respond. Our community has a right to know the type of neighbors buying property. Y'all remember that developer from last year. He tried to sweet talk the mayor and city council into letting him build a bunch of low rent, substandard, apartment complexes so they could house a bunch of Syrian refugees. Then the braggart claimed the government was going to subsidize the whole project. Remember how that turned out?"

Lily felt more confident hearing Mary Lou state this.

Valerie shuddered. "Eww. He didn't have a line on any homeless refugees. He planned to lease it to the state corrections agency to store their inmate overflow. Just the sex offenders and underage narcotic traffickers. A half-way house for the criminally insane. Ugh!"

LouEllen's face cringed, and her lips puckered. "Yeah, that was pretty creepy and a real close call."

Agitated, Mary Lou waved her hands in the air. "Vigilance is required to protect our citizens from this kind of trailer trash infesting our community. Has everyone forgotten how long it took us to get rid of that shabby trailer park south of the city near the reservoir? My in-laws joked saying it looked like the county garbage dump with all those old tires on each trailer to hold 'em down in high winds. Nothing we did improved the situation until that tornado ripped through Jarrell and plowed right down the middle. I felt sorry for them folks. But God said it was time to clear the path."

"You're not suggesting it was divine intervention that leveled that trailer park, are you?" Valerie asked.

Mary Lou shrugged and looked up, conveying as much innocence as was possible for her age.

Valerie snorted and insisted, "Society is based on laws and fair rulings. We must use the legal infrastructure to get at the truth of what's going on, then challenge where it's outside of the regulations. We've gone to Chief Jager and even Sheriff Blanton. They don't want any part of this."

Mary Lou's face contorted into an angry sneer the shade of a chili pepper. "That's right. Law enforcement around here thinks if you haven't broken any laws, you can get away with anything!"

"Imagine," LouEllen sarcastically placated. "You've got to break the law before anyone will help. What a world we live in."

Mary Lou glared at LouEllen. Lily stood ready to intercept if their needling one another escalated.

"Folks need awareness of the situation," Caroline interjected. "If they see or hear any specifics on the topic, we gotta get 'em on this show. We know there're rules to play by. But we don't roll over, ignore a problem, and meekly take what's dished out. Our freedoms, heck, our way of life, comes from an involved attitude and a willingness to fight for our beliefs. My husband believed in our constitutional rights, and I believe in the same values."

"We're sorry for your loss, Caroline," Lily whispered in a respectful tone.

Jo quietly asked, "Lily, what do they mean?"

"Caroline's husband joined the U.S. military after that horrific attack on our country in 2001. He died while in the service."

Jo blushed and shuffled her feet awkwardly until JJ took her hand and let her know with his silent, compassionate look, it was all okay.

Lily patted Jo's arm after seeing the exchange. "It's alright, child."

JJ motioned with a toss of his head that it was time to go upstairs, and Jo nodded.

Lily observed Jo scanning the small audience outside when she moved toward the stairs. Jo's gaze stopped on a man next to a young teen. Lily didn't recognize either of them. Jo's eyes met those of the girl, who reflected a flash of fear in her expression. Lily considered asking what was going on when JJ tugged on Jo's arm, and said, "Come on, honey."

Jo squeezed his hand and smiled at him. Jo looked back outside as the couple started up the stairs, but the teen, and maybe her father, were gone. Lily felt a wave of unease when their eyes met before Jo refocused on JJ as they ascended.

CHAPTER FOUR

Passionate Dusk 'til Dawn

The night passed all too quickly for the two young lovers from his perspective. JJ woke recalling each gentle caress and savored sensation. He loved their evening of simple pleasures starting with bathing in the oversized tub, exchanged rubdowns with scented lotion, and sweet lovemaking that left them satiated and entwined. He loved holding her in his arms until sleep overtook them—a perfect ending for a pair in love. The sunrise brought a rosy glow to their bedroom as sleep gave way to her open eyes and snuggles.

"Was there something you wanted to tell me last night, Jo? I sensed something was nagging at you as we came upstairs, but we got so delightfully distracted I forgot to ask. Did I do something?"

Jo chuckled and moved a bit closer under the covers. "No, honey, not you. I saw something that's hard to explain. This teenaged girl was standing next to an older man whom I assumed was her father. Something felt awkward, JJ, like she was scared almost looking for a way out. I was uncomfortable with the scene, but I can't tell you why. When I turned to look again, they were gone. It was odd."

"Jo, you picked this up looking through a window toward the late afternoon sun after mere seconds. I'm sorry you were shaken. There could be many reasons for an icy, frictional state between a father and daughter, like if she was dating someone such as me. I know you have the women's intuition advantage over emotionally challenged guys, but it was likely nothing."

"I guess you're right. I was tired after our travel. That podcast was interesting though. Those ladies seem to care about their community, but they are a bit opinionated, aren't they?"

"I'd have to agree with that statement. I can't resolve in my mind why their machines were hosed up."

"I know it'll come to you at some point. I'm hungry. Let's get dressed and go to breakfast."

"Race you to the tub."

Jo playfully pushed him. "Ladies first," she announced. "I think we ought to hike around and see what we can discover about Magnolia Bluff."

She rose from bed and JJ joined her, wrapping her in his arms. "Great idea. Hurry, otherwise, we might never leave this room."

"We might also try horseback riding. I love doing that at home when time permits. I bet Lily would know of riding options. This is such a quaint community. I want to see all it has to offer, okay?"

"Let's explore everything." He kissed her sweetly. "With our limited time, I'd like to enjoy the local color while we regain closeness for fun and play. I know that you brought those short shorts, but if we're going riding, you'll want your jeans. You're experienced enough that sneakers should work."

"I stuffed them and my bikini in my small backpack just in case. I know I'm not here for a film shoot, so ponytail and light-weight stuff is my plan. I'm ready to have some relaxing fun."

"No crash helmet or parachute?" JJ laughed as he twirled her around with a hug, then set her down and released her as he dashed off. Jo raced after JJ, who promptly grabbed the bathroom and locked the door. "Ah, I get the bathroom first."

Her comment, filled with palpable annoyance, penetrated through the door. "You tricked me, JJ."

CHAPTER FIVE

New Day Dawning

JJ enjoyed the long legs of his lady love as she preceded him down the hall, already planning their nighttime activities. The walk downstairs carried the heady aroma of muffins or sweet breads, plus the unmistakable scent of bacon that all made his mouth water.

"Jo, I wasn't hungry in our room, except for you, but now, I think I could eat a horse."

Jo looked over her shoulder and grinned. "I know, right? The smell is so strong it's making my stomach growl." She skipped down the stairs faster.

"Sweetheart, I think we're in for breakfast bonus calories we won't soon forget."

"And boy, am I glad, I burn 'em up fast."

Lily greeted them at the arch to the dining room. The screen door had a breeze flowing through, adding a touch of floral scent. "You two are just in time. I have a few guests this morning, but I reserved the corner table for you lovebirds. You can just take your time," she added as she showed the way. "I serve a variety of Texas breakfast favorites and can make just about anything. I suspect neither of you have any food allergies or dislikes or you'd have mentioned them when you checked in. Folks are usually particular about food they can't eat. Sunday breakfast is usually my way unless you say otherwise."

The tables were multiple shades of green with flowered cushioned seats. An artsy pot with a violet plant displaying light purple blooms sat in the middle of each table.

"I think Lily should go for it, don't you, Jo?"

"Yes, I like that idea to." Sitting Jo added, "Lily, this is so quaint. I love the violets."

"They're my favorite though I change out the plants in here a few times during the year. Now, help yourselves to your favorite beverage from the sideboard." She gestured. "I'll launch the delectable hallmark Sunday morning breakfast."

Lily turned with a grin and proceeded toward the swinging door to the kitchen when the front main phone rang causing her to alter course.

"Jo, can I get you juice or coffee?" JJ asked, as he stood.

"Just coffee for right now, thanks, honey."

He went to the left side of the self-serve area and grabbed two mugs. Each had different flowers imprinted on the outside. He switched out one with a rose pattern he knew Jo would adore. He picked up the pot to pour and couldn't help but overhear Lily from the desk outside the archway.

"Gus, why are you calling at this time of the morning? You know it's Sunday breakfast, and I'm busy— What? What kind of threatening email? My sign doesn't say Flower B&B plus bail bonds or bounty hunting. If you're getting threats, call the police, for heaven's sake!…No, don't do that, Gus! We need to keep pressure on these newcomers, acting like we aren't good enough to meet and greet. DO NOT cancel tomorrow's podcast!"

JJ poured coffee in the cups and looked around at the other guests keeping to themselves on the side. Maybe they couldn't hear her, he thought. He decided to pour juice for he and Jo as well as he kept listening to Lily's side of the call.

"I understand the threat. Hell, I had one, too. Mine threatened my prominent female appendages in a vice. Didn't happen 'cos I stood my ground and didn't wimp out. Grow a pair and see this through...Good. Talk later."

Lily turned and caught the eye of JJ as he frowned at her then picked up the beverages and returned to the table. She scurried through the arches and the swinging door to get the promised breakfast started.

"JJ, what's up?" Jo asked.

JJ leaned in and softly replied, "I'm not sure, but something isn't right." He glanced at two men in ranch clothing at the far end of the dining room. He had an idea. Winking at Jo, he asked, "Sweetheart, how do you like the coffee? It's so fresh." He nodded and grinned.

"It's almost as good as the coffee in Brazil. After we eat, can we go explore."

"Yep. Let me ask these guys if they can provide some ideas." He called over, "Hey, gentlemen. We're visiting town on a small vacation. Do you know where we can rent a couple of horses and find some good trails?"

The one in the black hat looked up and over his friend's shoulder. "No, señor. *Nostrums no hablamos ingles.*"

Jo brightened and turned around. "*Buenos días, necesitamos alquilar unos caballos para dar la vuelta al campo.*"

The man shook his head, peeled off money, and placed it on the tabletop as he stood. He jerked his head toward his buddy and they filed out. As the man reached their table, he leaned down to JJ's ear. "We don't like strangers either, son." He slapped JJ's back as he left.

JJ started to rise when Lily intercepted him with plates in hand. "Young man, sit. They ain't worth your time."

"Lily, I didn't mean to offend your guests. I simply asked if they knew about renting horses. I was trying to strike up a friendly conversation, but they stood and left as though I insulted them."

Lily shook her head in disgust. "Ah, that would be the surly one. The other doesn't speak at all. Never mind them. They keep to themselves and only snap at you when they want something. They come through every now and then. Their attitudes are as dependable as Texas heat in the summertime." She laughed and added, "The container on the left is the Canadian Maple syrup I get from a regular guest. The one on the right is our local pecan syrup which has a touch of pecan whiskey. I wouldn't recommend drowning your pancakes in it unless you want them to sit up and bark. If you forget which one is which, just sniff. You'll know."

JJ and Jo exchanged you-go-first looks. JJ relented after tasting the maple one. "I must try it. You said we wanted to experience this place, right?"

Jo smiled as he took off the top and inhaled. "Whoa! This smells like smooth liquor with a hint of pecans and sweetness. I'm passing on this to make certain I stay in the saddle."

"Lily, come sit with us a while, when you get a break," JJ said.

Lily returned with a plate of pancakes for them to share, then rushed over to pocket the money from the men's table. No other guests were present so she pulled up an extra chair.

"Lily," Jo said, "All of this is delicious. The bacon is perfectly crunchy."

JJ nodded and cleared his throat. "Sorry to have overheard your conversation, but it sounded weird from this side." JJ sampled a bit of the fluffy eggs. "You sounded angry. We're here on holiday, but I'd hate to sit idly by when nice people are threatened. Did you talk to the police?"

Jo leaned in and patted Lily's hand as if offering sympathy.

Lily spat with a sneer. "Police Chief Jager said take the complaint to the FBI 'cause they do all that computer stuff. He hates our podcast because we didn't use him as our announcer. County Sheriff Blanton is usually too busy getting his boots shined to even take my call. Our law enforcement thinks we old ladies exaggerate and shouldn't be using computers we don't understand. They think high tech is Velcro and Teflon."

"Are you saying the hack and slash yesterday wasn't the first time?"

Lily wailed and dabbed at her eyes with a tissue she pulled from her apron. "Exactly. It started when our podcast led with the new buyers in town that won't socialize with us locals. We've been doing podcasts for quite some time on different community events and other activities in nearby towns. We're getting an audience of folks dialing in to hear it live or just showing up at the location. Right when we latched on to this topic after we researched, we started receiving anonymous emails saying *drop the inquisition.* 'Course we ignored that and set up this ten-day circuit to various shopkeepers to get community support for businesses and helping find out what's going on out there. Then it got nasty. Guess they thought we thumbed our noses at them, which we did. Vulgar notes were found at each of our doorsteps one morning that were ugly, but the threat of physical violence is new to the last two broadcasts, and now Gus. The computer virus you fixed was the only one that could have shut down the show."

Lily jumped up and went for the coffeepot. Jo and JJ enjoyed the food. JJ looked at her. "Oh, honey, I'm sorry. Here I'm talking shop, and your breakfast got cold."

"It's okay if you can help Lily and her friends, JJ."

Lily refilled each of their cups.

"Lily, how about we pick this discussion up later? I promised Jo a fun day today. She'd really like to take a ride and explore."

Smiling, Lily looked delighted. "Fear not. I've got friends that will rent you some sweet horses and point you to the right trails. Some areas around the reservoir aren't fenced off. I'll call Hank, while you finish. Thank you for listening, young man."

"Just call me JJ."

CHAPTER SIX

Can't or Won't Help

Lily's eyes twinkled when she handed JJ the notes with the directions. "It's a short drive but easiest if you follow the directions. Don't trust your GPS. I haven't trusted them ever since the military began their experiments on weaponizing the SATCOM networks. I read that once satellite communication carriers get infected the despicable bad actors misinform people for sport. Any poor fool who trusts their GPS device deserves to aimlessly wander like Moses in the desert. We had some UT Austin astronomy students show up wanting to see the old Nike missile site. It's way south of Austin. Talk about green beans not knowing north from south. Sheesh!"

JJ felt the blush rise from his neck, recalling their delayed arrival due to GPS misdirection but shook it off, grateful Jo didn't intercept. "For somebody running a bed and breakfast, you seem to know a great deal about satellite communications and GPS poisoning. Are you with the Federal Witness protection program, and this is your new identity?"

Lily heartily laughed. "Young man, I can't reveal my past. If I did that I'd have to move and start over. I'm too plum old to start over. Besides I like meeting guests like you and Jo."

Not quite sure what to think, JJ read the note. He handed it to Jo with a small grin. He read it. "Ma'am, is this cursive writing?"

Lily cracked up. "I tend to write cursive because most young folks can't read it anymore. Har! Har! I'm done funning. I'll text you the directions but keep this as a reminder."

JJ patted her on the arm with affection. "Ms. Lily, my mom taught me to read and write cursive just for this type of circumstance."

Still grinning, Lily added, "You're a smart kid. Good upbringing, too. You'll come to several fences on this property so look for the gate with the welcome sign. Please secure the gate once you are inside. Our motto is, leave gates the way you find 'em."

"Ms. Lily, we won't embarrass you. Hank knows we're coming, right?"

"Correct. If you get lost on the way to the south end of the reservoir, ask someone for help. If they tell you go to the last stop sign and turn left, go ask someone else. Some Magnolia Bluff folks can't help but tease strangers with funny accents."

"I don't think I have a funny accent," said Jo.

"Child, do come along. Where you come from, I have the funny accent. When I was about eight or nine, my folks took us to see my aunt and uncle in Houston. They had one daughter Kathy, but we hit it off right away. But after a couple of hours of playing, Kat stood back with her arms crossed for a moment then announced, *Y'all talk funny.*"

"I like that story. When we get back, can we watch the older podcast shows? Jo wanted to see them, and I'd like to verify the content to the timing of the threatening emails. Did you keep those? They might have some interesting tidbits of information as well."

Lily beamed. "I like knowing that you're taking an interest in our problem. Don't put yourself crosswise with your beautiful lady. I thought you two wanted to deeee-compress?"

Jo chuckled. "Lily, we're here for rest and relaxation. Honestly, I'm enjoying being involved. I don't get to see him work. I'm finding it fascinating."

JJ grabbed Jo's hand. "Come on, you, let's get on with our riding. We'll have plenty of time to deeee-compress later."

Hank provided two delightful horses, Midnight and Lucy. He requested they be returned in about four hours. JJ and Jo easily mounted and took off at a steady pace following the trail.

"JJ, aren't these flowers beautiful? I could get lost in all the colors."

"Honey, you could never get lost in the colors, you're too pretty. Let's follow this to the reservoir trail and find a place to snack on the sandwiches Hank's wife provided."

"Okay. It was nice of her to go to that trouble for strangers."

The water was as smooth as the air was still. "Look, Jo," JJ pointed, "did you see that fish jump?"

Jo giggled. "No, but I bet that blue heron did. Watch him." Moments later the heron snagged his wiggling snack and took off.

"Wow. I'm glad we saw that. Wish I'd caught a photo."

"We need to keep our phones handy to capture these memories. There's a spot to the right with a couple of boulders near the edge of the water. The trees behind there have shade and it looks like some grass for the horses. Midnight deserves a break."

"You're right, Jo. Lucy's a sweetie. Can you set up lunch? I'll get the horses tethered after they take a drink."

Jo skinned down to her bikini while JJ completed his tasks, distracted by her every move.

JJ whistled and walked to where she set up the picnic. "Is your plan to eat first then a little swim?"

Jo gave him a hug. "After a hug and a kiss, yep, but let's take a quick swim first so we can dry in the sun before redressing to ride."

"Good plan."

The water was a refreshing delight. They splashed and played, then ate the sandwiches and cookies. "Jo, those chocolate chip cookies hit the spot. Let's get dressed and see if we can locate the trail Lily suggested to see the wall of shame. We need lots of photos."

They dressed, mounted the horses, and headed toward the back trail on the map. The trail was well worn, so they felt confident. They took pictures of the sights including each other.

The sun angled to around two o'clock. Jo checked her phone time and nodded. "JJ, where exactly are we? The map the outfitters gave us doesn't show this road or that locked gate."

"You're right. My phone is out of power from all the photos and tracking. I wish I had a USB port on this saddle for charging. I think I can retrace our path. If we cross here on this smaller patch, we could cut across then loop back to Hank's place. If I'm right, it's shorter, too."

"Hey, there's a car headed toward us on the road next to our trail. Let's flag them down and ask. I'd hate to waste time crossing the road just to double back. I'd rather get off this saddle sooner than later."

"I hear you, babe. I'm getting sore, too."

JJ dismounted and waved, but the driver passed him, drove to the gate, and stopped. JJ walked the horse up to the driver, who was using a key to unlock the gate. "Sir, hi."

The man had a swarthy complexion and longish hair under his cowboy hat. A large stain showed on his back—undoubtedly sweat. JJ noticed his worn boots and suspected he wasn't the owner.

"Excuse me, are you the owner?"

The man turned. His eyes narrowed as his lips curled into a scowl. "I'm just hired help. This is private property! Keep moving, or I'll call the police."

The lock disengaged, and the gate swung wide. The man stomped back to his truck, raising a small dusty cloud in his wake. He got in, shut the door, and punched the gas pedal. The dusty grey Ford F-250 lurched through the opening, throwing up gravel and dust, slightly startling Lucy, and momentarily blinding JJ. When his eyes cleared, the gate was locked, and the vehicle gone.

He heard Jo walking behind him, and the two horses nickered. Jo said, "He wasn't helpful or friendly. Let's walk the horses for a ways so our muscles can recover." JJ sighed with relief. Jo asked, "What did he say when you asked for directions?"

"The guy snapped that we were trespassing and to leave. It reminded me of the attitude from those men this morning. Jo, your intuition is typically good. Something's fishy, or at least dusty. Let's get back to Flower and dig a little."

Jo beamed and nuzzled him before they retraced their steps.

CHAPTER SEVEN

A Polaroid Selfie

JJ dismounted and felt twinges in his thighs reminding him to ride more often. Thoughts of a nice soak with Jo later crossed his mind. JJ handed the horses' reins to Hank. "Hank, thanks for loaning us your two gentle riding animals."

Jo caressed Midnight's muzzle. "A lovely treat to slow down and enjoy the countryside from the back of a horse. Would you please take a picture of us? I'd like a keepsake of our time here."

Hank grinned and extended his gnarled hand. "Give me your Polaroid camera and I'll be happy to, young lady."

Jo looked confused.

JJ smiled, opened his mobile device to camera, and handed it to the rancher. "We'd like you to use this, if you don't mind." He turned around the screen and mimicked the process. "Look through here and press this button. We didn't bring our Polaroid."

Before Hank could take the gag any further, a commanding voice announced, "Give me the phone. I'll do it."

JJ handed his cellphone over to the uniformed female with her dark brown hair pulled into a tight ponytail. Her emblems tagged her as a Texas Game Warden. JJ noted her height at near 5'10" with eyes that matched the cloudless sky. "I'd hate to interrupt your work, ma'am, but thank you."

"I'm not that busy, young man, we are in the middle of God's country. Thank you for a bit of respite." She extended her hand to shake. "Madison Jackson's the name." She turned slightly stomped her foot and glared at Hank. "Why do you pull that same worn-out old gag of using a Polaroid for pictures? I've only ever seen them in museums and antique stores. No one in this generation realized those cameras used instant development films. When folks used 35mm they had to wait for a company to develop your memories. So, stop it." She turned and sighted the frame. "Alright you two, bring the horses in closer… There, that's it."

Hank chuckled. "I was having a bit of sport. I like teasing young people. Madison, you're too serious."

JJ and Jo smiled at the exchange. JJ suspected she and Hank were great friends. He wondered if they might be related.

"My name's JJ, Ms. Jackson, and this is my girlfriend, Jo. We took no offence at all. I find teasing is often acceptance. Midnight and Lucy provided us a great ride around the countryside, a nice swim in the reservoir, and a picnic lunch. Nearly a perfect day."

"Warden Jackson, thank you for taking a couple of photos." Jo smiled. "I like them better than arms-length selfies."

Madison grumbled. "You two knock it off with the Ms. this and warden that. Please call me Madison like everyone does. Everyone but Hank here. He keeps calling me *Buff and Guns* behind my back."

Hank closed his eyes as if hiding as his skin tone turned beet red.

JJ, to save Hank, said, "Warden…er, Madison, you look remarkably fit and trim in your uniform. Do you work out daily?"

Jo turned her face toward JJ and delivered a withering non-verbal dressing down with her eyes. JJ knew she was right and touched her hand in acknowledgement.

Madison smirked. "Let's move on before we make this couple mad on their vacation. You two rode out south of the reservoir. Did you see anything unusual?"

"Like what, Madison?" asked Jo. "We've never been here. The horseback ride gave us a new perspective of the Texas countryside."

JJ intervened, "Ma'am, we came across a surly pickup driver. He got angry when we asked for directions."

"JJ's right, he floored that F250 through the gate tossing up a cloud of dust. The dust here tastes awful."

JJ recounted the events of that meeting. Madison commented, "Some folks hate their privacy invaded."

Hank grumbled unintelligibly and snorted. "True, but their eight-foot fences wreak havoc on the deer habits. I was making money with my deer leases, but this season—no way. The animals will reroute, but not through my land. Lately, every time we set up for outdoor cooking, Mateo's workers run a bunch of trucks over that blasted dirt road sending dust through my back pasture, into my pergola and my bar-b-que. I swear they wait for the wind to shift to aggravate me."

JJ paused just in case there was more Hank wanted to share. JJ breathed a sigh of relief. "We need to head back to Magnolia Flower."

Madison's eyebrows arched high. "You're at Flower? By chance were you the one that helped get Mary Lou's PC back online for her podcast?"

JJ felt his face heating with slight embarrassment. "You heard about that? Wow, news travels fast here."

"We do have an impressive gossip-vine in Magnolia Bluff. Doesn't take a genius to get sucked into the noise. I've always wanted to know more about computers. I couldn't keep track of the permits or the violators around here without that resource.

There's never enough time to up my skills about the available technology. I need to before my job gets done by artificial intelligent machines on computers."

Jo tugged on JJ. "Whoa, look at the time. We need to get back. Thanks again for the horses. Come on, Jo."

CHAPTER EIGHT

The Light of Your Eyes

JJ parked near the front of Magnolia Flower. He walked around and opened the door for Jo. She interlaced their fingers as they held hands. They dreamily exchanged thoughtful glances and smiles as they approached the stairs. He hoped they were on the same relaxation wavelength.

JJ grinned at her pretty face, framing it with his hands. He added one swift kiss and suggested, "How about we take a nice relaxing bath, followed by a massage with that nice lotion you brought? I can promise your tired muscles a sensual journey that will deliver a wonderful nap before we hunt for an exquisite dinner."

Jo nodded with her eyes lowered, and they walked up the steps to the entrance. JJ opened the front door and they stepped into a boiling caldron of raised voices and shrieks.

"LouEllen, please calm down," Lily admonished. "You can't rush in here breathing hard with your heart condition, still sporting those extra pounds you promised you'd lose. LouEllen, this isn't going to help. I don't want to be calling an ambulance again."

LouEllen bawled, "Lily, we both got those emails telling us not to do anymore podcasts on the new residents. We tried talking to Mary Lou, but she just gets that funny glint in her eyes and says, 'We've got them on the run now.' Please help us! If the podcast doesn't go on, she can still pay her bills. For her it's the prestige. Mary Lou doesn't have a business like you and me that pay our living expenses."

Jo looked over the tops of her sunglasses at JJ, who took in the exchange. He understood her petition to offer help to these women. He resolutely sighed, knowing his plans were postponed. "Ladies, we couldn't but overhear the consternation in your frightfully high-pitched tones. Can we help?"

Lily melted with relief as her features relaxed. Grabbing her friends by their elbows she herded them into the parlor to the right of the doorway. The ladies quickly recounted the problems as JJ called upon each.

"May I see the threatening emails, please? Lily, you also said you received at least one. I'd like to see that as well. You've asked for help from the local police, right? I don't want to get crosswise with your law enforcement folks." He turned and made a face at Jo who politely smiled.

"LouEllen," Lily directed, "Caroline, get your laptops and bring them back here for JJ to study while I show him my emails."

"Jo, hon, would you mind getting mine from our room so I can access my digital tools if needed, please?" Jo scampered off. "You're an angel," JJ called.

Lily pulled JJ into her modest office and signed into email. JJ read the digital threads which included the police responses. He searched her face for any hidden secrets and saw none.

"May I forward these to my email account?" JJ asked. "I have some computer forensic tools that I can use. As soon as LouEllen and Caroline arrive, we'll repeat it for them. I presume the threats are from the same source. That will provide me some leads, unless there are additional details you need to share."

Jo returned with his laptop, and he connected, grabbing each of the messages. He launched a program that spilled everything out on the screen in SMTP binary code.

Watching his every move and the screen, Lily asked, "What're you doing? How come the email has gone from readable to gibberish?"

Not moving his gaze from the screen, he explained. "We call this a digital microscope. The sender didn't sign the email or show their address, but the underlying code contains the *from* and *to* information that allowed delivery. Since I have all three emails, I can look for...and there it is. Not a bad cloaking exercise." He mumbled, "Nowhere near the APT goons I typically hunt."

"Uh, APT, what's that?" Caroline asked.

JJ, still reading the screen, clarified, "Advanced Persistent Threats. In the cyber security world, all known cyber scum is APT plus a number as a shorthand in our communications with other digital hunters."

JJ's fingers glided across the keyboard. He wished his hands were otherwise engaged like running all over Jo's skin. The scent of her perfume teased his nose.

JJ hopped up and faced the circle behind him. "Ladies, I'd appreciate you not repeating anything I say about my work against bad actors on the internet. I know your podcast is all about gossip, but I would like you to maintain confidentiality for anything you might see.

"Lily, you claimed that there are recordings of the podcasts. We'd like to watch them to see if we can spot anything unusual. The correlation between the topics you discuss on these shows and the email threats might not be obvious. Can we access them from here?"

LouEllen brightened. "I have access to the archives. Let me show you where to begin. If you want, I can give you admin access to the files."

JJ looked up and smiled at Jo. "Honey, come help me watch these? Two sets of eyes are always better than one."

With a mischievous smile, Jo coyly joked, "You need the bright light of my eyes to study? Sure."

"Girls, I don't think they need our help to watch," Lily announced. "We've got errands to run. Let's let them work without our hot breath on their necks."

JJ chuckled. "Thanks, Lily. We'll note any questions in case we need your clarification."

"I hate to miss anything," LouEllen complained, "but it feels like watching paint dry. Come on, Caroline, let's leave them to it."

JJ snapped his head around. "Ladies, just because we're looking for clues doesn't mean the threat is gone. I know this is your town, but you need to be situationally aware. Be vigilant. They know who you are, which puts you at an extreme disadvantage. Stay on guard until I can get some answers."

It was a sobering declaration for the women. Lily nodded at the gravity of their situation. "Thank you, JJ, for jumping into this mess."

Lily turned to her friends. "I recommend we go back to packing in case we get caught unawares. LouEllen, I know you have a weapon. Caroline, how about you?"

Caroline nodded, her eyes a bit darker, and a grim shadow crossed her face.

"JJ, holler if you find something," Lily said as she left with her buddies.

CHAPTER NINE

Coloring the Picture

The next two hours passed slowly viewing the recorded podcasts. Jo held JJ's hand while the exercise continued. "Ow. Jo, you're squeezing too hard, hon. What's the matter?"

JJ caught Jo's wild-eyed look. His alarm rose as she pointed at the screen and gasped. "JJ, back it up. More. Back it up. There. Start from there, slow. See? Stop and hold the image. That girl looks like the one I saw when we arrived." Jo's eyes filled with tears, threatening to spill as she croaked, "I know where I've seen that fear, JJ! Monica looked at me just like that before she ran at the compound fence. We knew we were captives. She'd made up her mind she couldn't stay. They took…I never saw her…" Jo sobbed into her palms.

JJ gathered her into his arms. "Jo, honey, you made it out, alive. Your parents died for you to be safe. You overcame the odds and fled that hell-hole. You're strong. You found us. You're safe now. No one can take your freedom. They'd have to get through me, and that's not an option. Come on now, let's figure this out."

Smiling through her tears, she sniffed, regaining her composure. "I know, sweetheart. She appears trapped, like a wounded animal. Her eyes are hollow as they dart about. I've read about human trafficking and thought that would have been my next adventure if I hadn't escaped. She's the right age like I was, and she appears to be searching for an opening. I'm probably wrong. Maybe I read too many stories during my last shoot, but the Texas border was mentioned often. I hope there's nothing bad happening. But if we find there is a threat, we need to help."

JJ nodded. "Yes, my love. Let's see if we can find a pattern in the rest of these recordings. If there's a similar issue with young women or t'weens like you just spotted, looking fearful, the emails make more sense. Help me look for more evidence. We don't want anyone entrapped in a physical or emotional prison." JJ backed up the recording and pointed to the screen. "Was there a guy like this one next to the teenager you saw yesterday?"

"Not the same man, but an icy expression like this one." She pointed. "Look at her hand, JJ. Her fingers are folded over and around her thumb. That's the universal sign for abductees or victims of domestic violence to signal for help. You see it in nearly every public restroom these days. I did when we stopped on our drive here. It's also all-over social media and went viral a couple of years ago. Looks like we may have two possibilities. I think I'm right on this being more than just a troubled kid."

JJ rocked back in his chair. "Alright, Jo. I trust your instincts, but remember, we need to prove any allegations. We aren't citizens of this country, and this might be coincidence. But one of my mentors, Dr. Quip, taught me coincidences are often highly engineered."

JJ grabbed his notebook and pen and handed it to Jo. "Can you start listing what we found? First, Magnolia Bluff has secretive folks who are buying property and won't answer any questions. Second, a highly spirited community podcast group complains about it on open mic that stirs up the community and publishes to their channel, which has thousands of followers.

Third, we see creepy types lurking around the podcasts with teenagers signing for help. Fourth, the podcasters get email threats to stop, and malware that locks up their equipment."

"What about the guys at breakfast and that man who snarled when you asked for help when we were riding near the reservoir." Jo added, "Are you annoyed that we came here to Magnolia Bluff to relax, de-compress, and disengage?"

"Babe, let's go find Lily and ask her for introductions to the police chief. I'd like to review what we uncovered. This is shaping up nastier than I imagined."

Jo grinned. "Only after I touch up my makeup. Silly tears marred my eyeliner."

JJ smiled and gently caressed Jo's face as he whispered, "We wouldn't want that now, would we? While you're doing that, I need to send an email to some folks I know to add some color to this puzzle. Meet you at the stairs."

"Lily, we'd like to see some of the records, what's the best way to get connected?"

Lily suggested JJ to speak to Daphne, owner of the Head Case and favorite hairdresser for most of the women of Magnolia Bluff. Lily promised Daphne had connections to everyone and dirt on most. "JJ, she's always polite when she gets her way, but vindictive with words and gossip if she feels slighted."

She directed JJ and Jo to use her walking directions for their first stop at the county records department.

They headed toward downtown, noting the older buildings with the worn stonework. "Jo, can you believe how these sidewalks aren't spoiled with trash. People waved or said hello as they passed."

"I know. The shops look inviting with clever displays, plants, and freshwater bowls for puppies. See the flowers against that old building? The butterflies seem to be dancing from one to the other."

"Yep. Even the birds on that manicured lawn appear busy grooming out the worms and extracting other tasty delights."

They found Daphne outside the building. "Hi. Let's go in and see if we can get a look at what you want."

"Hi Daphne. I'm JJ and this is Jo. Thanks for helping with introductions so we can speed up our research. Sorry we're a little late. You've got a pretty town."

"No problem, you're tourists. Call me Daphne." Daphne pointed to the door they wanted. "I've been here a couple of times. It's tough even for me, living in this town, to get copies. It'd be worse than horrible if I didn't help. I expect old Wiley E. Purloin has greased the palm of the county clerk with some simoleons to discourage nosey folks."

Jo asked, "Simoleons? What are they?"

JJ chuckled. "That, my dear, is slang for money. Daphne is suggesting that the county clerk and records keeper is getting hush money or a bribe."

Once inside, the three of them marched up to the records desk. JJ wondered if this clerk could be corrupt.

The clerk raised her head and frowned. "You again? What'd you do, round up an audience to help ruin my day? You might as well go 'cause the copier's broken. I'm closing in twenty minutes."

JJ smiled. "Ma'am, no copy needed. My name is JJ and we got involved in a crazy debate. I just want to confirm a couple of details. Won't be but a minute." He gestured with his thumb. "I want to prove Daphne here is incorrect about any strange activity. If you'll let me see the primary contract that Wiley E. Purloin of the Cheatham, Pilferus, and Pocketum Law Firm registered on behalf of Superior Import and Export, I can show her in seconds. Then, we'll get out of your way. Heck, I'll even buy you a beer later in thanks. I know I'm right."

Daphne opened her mouth to protest, and her eyes narrowed. Jo squeezed her hand below the view of the clerk. JJ's ploy got the desired effect.

The clerk almost chuckled. Shooting a smirk toward Daphne, she halted her ledger entries and ambled over to a file cabinet to retrieve the Deed of Record book. She placed it on the counter. "I've dragged the damn thing out for so many people, I know exactly how to retrieve it in my sleep. You have eighteen minutes before I'm locking the doors from the outside."

Daphne snapped, "I know you're glad you do your own hair. There is nothing I could do for it, Gladys."

JJ grabbed the book, walked over to a table, and pulled Daphne close to his side. He signaled Jo to go to the other side of the table and handed her his cell. They established an assembly line to flip the pages while Jo snapped photo after photo.

"See, Daphne, it's right there," JJ said, with a raised voice, pointing to a blank spot on the page and winking at her. "You're pestering these folks for no reason." He flipped the book closed and picked it up, turning toward the counter. He handed it back. "Thank you, ma'am. We're done. You have the luxury of ten extra minutes to yourself. I'll make certain there's credit in your name for a beer at the bar across the way."

Inside the car, JJ said, "Thanks again for helping. I saw a place that's questionable, but I want to send it to a friend of mine. Research is a hobby of ours."

"You ready to visit Police Chief Jager," Daphne asked, "better known as Chief Tommy?"

"I'm ready. I've got my letter of introduction from Lily, but how should I address the Police Chief? Chief Tommy seems informal." Jo nodded her agreement.

Daphne laughed. "You could do what I always do and say *your reverence* when speaking to him."

"He likes that term?"

"Not exactly. He threatens to shove his boot up my butt for being insolent."

"Good to know. I'll stick to Chief."

Tough Audience

JJ held Jo's hand as they entered the police office connected to the back of the courthouse.

Jo looked up at the weathered exterior of the building with the clock. Snapping a photo, she commented. "JJ, this building is magnificent, and the clock on top matches the time on my phone. I wonder how often they set it."

"I don't know. I suspect the clock's mechanical movement, when it was installed, was that good. Did you know that to have a clock tower in Texas was a mark of a civilized county? Many of those received restoration as a part of Texas history preservation. One article I read indicated the town leaders worked to outdo the clocks and towers of adjacent counties. Almost like a competition. Not an inexpensive town investment either."

"Wow, I had no idea." Jo inhaled the sweet floral scents carried on the breeze. "I thought Texas was supposed to smell like livestock. I bet they have full-time gardeners."

"I suspect you're right, Jo. Do you think the town decorates for the seasons, too? The walkway around back leads to the offices of Chief Jager, from what Daphne said. If we have time after our discussion, let's sneak a peek inside the courthouse."

"Deal."

They opened the door to find a slight-built lady in uniform plucking away on her computer. A quick smile from the brown-eyed brunette was accompanied by a greeting. "Good afternoon, how may I help you?"

JJ replied, "My name is JJ. This is my girlfriend, Jo. We'd like to speak to Chief Jager, if he's in."

"He's in. Hey, Tommy, have a couple of folks out here who want to speak to you."

A deep raspy voice replied from the open doorway at the far end of the room. "Send 'em back, Gloria."

Jo grinned. "Thank you, Gloria. Sorry to interrupt your work."

"It's not a problem, ma'am. I'm finishing a burglary report from the café for the theft of half a dozen donuts. Nothing critical. Tommy is usually out here too, but he was finishing his lunch. Don't let him buffalo y'all."

JJ grabbed Jo's hand and proceeded to the door, tapping gently on the doorjamb.

"Well, don't just stand there. Come in, take a seat."

JJ noted the man's broad shoulders, chiseled features on his squarish face, with a head of thick wavy black hair, and grey eyes taking the measure of him and Jo. "Thank you, Chief Jager, for taking the time to see us."

"Just call me Tommy. Most everyone else does. You visitin' Magnolia Bluff?"

"We are," JJ replied, thinking this lawman seemed sincere. "We're staying at Flower. There were some issues with their podcasts that we corrected, but I wanted to bring them to your attention."

Tommy laughed. "Those, um…mature ladies are as gossipy as it gets in this town. If something isn't happening to stir folks up, they start something new to keep the excitement going. Father Gorman, Gunther Fight, and I have tried to solve their issues for years. Gorman is a preacher in town and Gunther is Mary Lou's husband. Once they get onto a new thing, the old one just vanishes like it never happened. Small town gossip is a way of life 'round here."

JJ saw Jo's frown out of the corner of his eye and realized she was about to jump in with her thoughts, so he preempted, "Sir, I'm not certain about other times, but I can prove the podcast threats are real and escalating."

Tommy folded his arms across his chest and leaned back in his chair that groaned at the movement. "Prove how, young man?"

"Please call me JJ. I run a security consulting company from my offices in São Paulo. I review private and public enterprise systems, resulting in fixing security breaches and locating origination sources. The ladies that do the shows and their location owners are getting frightening emails. There are also a couple hacker instances on two laptops and a router that I patched."

Tommy arched his eyebrow and cocked his head to one side. "Can you show me your proof, young man?"

Jo handed over some documents while JJ explained, "These show some of the information I found, and the nature of the threats."

"Did you discover who sent them?"

"Not yet, but the Ladies of Magnolia podcasters are nervous. Even Gus at the hardware store was warned via email not to go on with today's podcast. Someone doesn't want their broadcasts to continue regarding the new folks who moved in and built a fence around a property that appears to have originally been open range."

Tommy shuffled through the papers, studying the notes JJ had made in the margins. "You don't know who sent them, but can you prove it wasn't Mary Lou? No one likes attention better than Ms. Fight. Y'all know that podcast is her baby. She yells at people when they say they don't listen. Before this, she ran the Crimson Hat Society until it failed, and she was injured. For years she's complained about so many things I could never prove. Nowadays her complaints go in one ear and out the other. Heck, Gloria is working a thief with a focus on sweets. That's a case we can solve. I'd rather stop a thief than grab at bits and bytes with no substantiation."

"Chief Jager," Jo complained, "I saw the fear in the eyes of your citizens, including Mary Lou. Their current situation might be different than marketing noise to drum up business."

"Ma'am," Tommy placated, "it might be, but unless I get some proof, I don't have the time or manpower to waste on conjecture. I'm sure you both have your hearts in the right place. But I've known these ladies nearly my whole life. They love to stir it up then chuckle later."

JJ rubbed his hand over his hair. "Alright, Chief. I get it. I'll leave these documents with you. If I find anything else, I'll let you know. As a side note, Jo and I rode some of Hank's horses near the reservoir yesterday. This is a lovely area, colorful and quiet. At least it was until we were trying to return to Hank's after getting on the wrong trail. A man pulled his grey Ford F-250 up to a gate and got out. I asked directions. He told me in clear language to leave and not return. He said, 'Strangers aren't welcome,' in a menacing tone. It surprised me. Until this point, Magnolia Bluff seemed friendly."

The chief jotted down a note on the papers JJ had provided. "Magnolia Bluff is a quiet friendly community. That man was likely one of the contractors brought in to do some specialized work. The nosy and the curiosity seekers are often frowned upon unless you've been introduced. No law was broken, but I'll keep it in mind."

Tommy rose and extended his hand to JJ, a clear signal that the meeting was over. JJ and Jo shook hands and thanked him for his time. They walked out, and Gloria immediately got Jo's attention with a wave of her fingers.

"Ma'am, the man in the Ford truck, what did he look like?"

Jo wrinkled her brow as if bringing his image front and center. "He was a little shorter than JJ but at least twenty pounds heavier. Rough facial hair like he neglected to shave. His worn jeans bagged around the seat, and his shirt was misbuttoned. He tied his oily black hair with a strip of leather. JJ, did I miss anything?"

"Only his voice, Jo, that you couldn't have heard from where you were. Gloria, his voice was gravelly like someone who smokes a lot or has a dry throat."

"Thank you, both. Ma'am," Gloria added with a grin, "I pegged you right. You're the observant one."

Jo grinned. "Gloria, is there a way we can walk inside the courthouse? I like older buildings, and this one is interesting."

"Sure. In fact, head out the door over here," she suggested, waving her hand to the right, pointing. "It'll take you up the stairs. Court isn't in session right now, but you can see the place. It's a historical landmark. I've loved wandering around this place since I was a kid. Closed doors however, locked or not, means keep out."

They both nodded and left by the side door.

CHAPTER ELEVEN

Up the Ante

JJ felt disappointed after the meeting with chief. He usually solved problems, but this one was a doozie. "Jo, let's head to the Hardware Store. With the podcast occurring there today we might learn something useful."

"JJ, he didn't seem concerned. Do you think he his hiding something?"

"Not really. He answered our questions. His reasoning was logical."

"You're right. Plus, Lily believes in him and his love for this community. Maybe she's a little sweet on him."

"Let's keep it in mind."

People were congregating near the store when JJ and Jo rounded the corner. They entered and greeted Gus with a handshake and waved to the podcast team standing to the side. JJ noted where things were placed, scanning for the exits.

"Gus seems distracted," Jo whispered. "JJ, is it me or does his face look a little green?"

"He looks like a teenager fidgeting around to delay asking for a first date. The sweat is beading up on his forehead as his eyes dart across the ladies connecting their equipment."

"Gus," Mary Lou called, "we need more space opened through the front window for folks to see our show in action."

"Don't fret so, Gus. We know you spend a great deal of time making the displays attractive to shoppers," LouEllen offered. "If you'll move the rakes and gardening plants for the show, we'll make sure to give an extra plug for your store. The audience likes seeing the speakers during the discussions. Once the show is over you can put everything back. Daphne can stay to help if you like."

Daphne nodded with a curled lip and moved, knocking over two plants that fell into the rakes, resulting in a noisy metallic crashing sound as the equipment hit the tiles. "Oops," she yelped.

"Never mind, Daphne," grumbled Gus. "Please, let me destroy the displays myself. Go be a podcaster and bring me more business."

"JJ, can you please help Gus move that large display to give us more room?" Lily suggested. "Jo, honey, we could use you for a mic test if you don't mind."

JJ smiled at Jo then watched her rush to assist while he helped Gus. He heard Jo's guidance, "Ladies, your lighting is creating shadows. It's not positioned to make you look your best. It needs to be more…" JJ turned in time to see Jo reposition the three light stands to brighten the faces of the hosts. "…like that."

Mary Lou eyed the others. "We didn't know we were doing it wrong. This ain't your first rodeo, sweetie, is it?"

Jo innocently grinned without missing a beat. "It's amazing what I learned in high school drama."

JJ caught Lily's eyes narrowing at the exchange. Mary Lou looked unconvinced. The alarm on Lily's phone chimed, announcing the ten-minute mark before the broadcast. "Alright, listen up," Lily advised. "We've got less than ten before show time. Pick up the pace. Father Gorman, are you about ready to lend us that rich whiskey voice to deliver the intro? We need this show to run as smooth as you sound. Gus, this show is gonna knock the socks off our community."

"Ladies, remember the outline we discussed," Mary Lou interjected. "I want to dive into it today. We're going to deliver more heat to the invaders. Let's saddle up and do this!"

"Thanks, son." Gus clapped JJ on the back. "I forgot how heavy my display was."

"Happy to help. Podcasters look delighted with the crowd gathering at the window. Before they start, would you show me the email you received? Lily mentioned it and showed me the ones she'd received. I'd like to view it on the device where you first got it. Please?"

Jo walked up and took JJ's hand, grinning. "That was kinda fun, JJ. Hi, Gus, I'm Jo. Are you okay? You look a little stressed."

"I'm okay." Gus shuffled from one foot to another as if weighing his options. He grunted. "JJ, are you some kind of detective, or just nosing into our business?"

"Fair question, Gus. I'm not a detective, but I like helping people with technological issues. Lily, Daphne, and LouEllen each received threatening emails. Officer Tommy is reluctant to get involved. In my work, computers are the weapons of choice. You don't have to show me what you got if you don't want to."

Gus nodded his head and turned toward the door behind the displays. JJ presumed it led to the backroom office as he followed. Gus mechanically logged into his email and pulled up the offending communication. Before giving the chair to JJ, he confessed, "I like those ladies out there. Mary Lou, not so much."

JJ quickly scanned the email. "May I forward it to my account? I need to examine this with my digital tools." Gus nodded.

JJ and Jo reached the door when familiar shrieks erupted from the broadcast area. JJ, followed by Jo and Gus, rushed to the table.

"Gus, we have no internet," Mary Lou shouted. "We can't go live! Didn't you pay your bill? All the connectivity is dead. No wi-fi means no podcast. Dammit."

JJ caught Jo's look and hurried in to analyze the problem.

"We were at the start time then…whoosh. No internet," Daphne lamented.

JJ accessed the machine. "Gus, what's the admin password for your wi-fi device?"

Gus stared blankly at JJ and mumbled, "The wi-fi has a password? I just plugged in the box I was shipped, and it worked."

JJ shook his head, and added, "Right. The default password wasn't changed. After we fix this, I'll show you how to change it so it won't be hacked. I'm in it." He looked at some information and stated, "Someone stopped your wi-fi using the default password. Let me reset it. Hopefully they didn't set up a DDOS attack, but I'll check."

"DDOS attack," LouEllen questioned, "what's that?"

JJ replied, not looking up from the monitor, "That's a distributed denial of service attack. Basically, it's caused by machines sending specialized data requests in huge numbers that can overwhelm a device, making it fail. Like a kid at the county fair having three cotton candy cones, two bags of popcorn, and ice cream. I'm sure you know what happens until that kid's system clears."

"Our show must go on," Mary Lou hissed. "JJ, have you got any other magic tricks in case what you're doing doesn't work?"

"Do any of you have a current generation smart phone? If you do, bring it to me and I'll set up a tethering end point to connect the internet. It's a stopgap."

Moments ticked by as JJ configured the phone.

Gus hollered, "The wi-fi device has restarted and has power, but all the lights show solid red."

JJ frowned. "Yeah. These guys aren't playing fair. It's going to take more time, and I need some additional equipment to fix it." He wondered who these guys were and how they trained. They were effective, but sloppy. "Ladies, tethering is your only option. It's not going to be a robust link. Once your show starts, tell the audience your show is under digital attack and apologize for the poor quality. I suggest you turn the show into a sermon about how your adversaries are trying to silence you. If this doesn't get you listenership, nothing will. You might mention that Gus is a hero for having the show here after receiving threats."

The system connected. LouEllen and Daphne let out whoops and hip-bumped with excitement.

True to form, Mary Lou nodded to Father Gorman. His calm voice did quick introductions and had everyone bow their heads and pray. After the Amen, Mary Lou nodded to JJ then smiled at the audience. She launched into a blistering verbal rampage for the show's followers. All three of the ladies were in rare form and highly animated in the show's heated debate.

Jo tugged on JJ's arm. "JJ, let's go outdoors to scan the crowd. Whoever hammered this show must have someone watching."

JJ smiled and kissed her cheek. "Agreed. I'm sure they are mad that the issue was overcome. Help me look for someone really aggravated at hearing the live show."

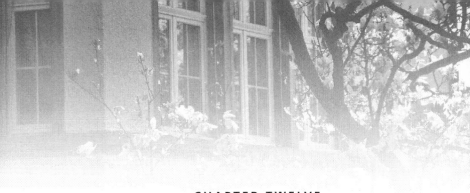

CHAPTER TWELVE

Alone at Last

Lily greeted Jo and JJ with quick hugs the next morning when they entered the dining room for breakfast. "You're godsends. After the miracle you pulled off at Gus's Hardware, how 'bout some champagne mimosas to start off your morning? I figure it's the least I can do as a small thank you for your support."

Jo beamed. JJ frowned. "Seems a little extravagant, Lily. We're helping your group. No biggie." He caught Jo's arched eyebrows and pleading eyes, topped off with a sweet smile, and chortled. "Alright. If I start dancing on the table, withdraw the bubbly. Lily, have the grumpy guys been in this morning, or have they already left?"

Lily raised her shoulders and tilted her head to one side. "They've already flown the coop. Paid the bill in cash and didn't say goodbye. Early too, like something was wrong."

Jo wrinkled her nose at Lily's comment. "There's nothing amiss with the food or accommodations here at Flower. I've enjoyed myself—immensely."

Lily rested her hand on Jo's shoulder. "Bless you, child. No. It's from their world. They didn't elaborate when I asked if they enjoyed their stay or if they'd give me a nice review. They didn't eat, and even turned down the sweet bread pastries and coffee

I offered for the road. It wouldn't bother me a bit to never see them again."

JJ chuckled. "We'll leave an agreeable review. I hope there are enough extra stars to use in the rating. Your accommodations and food are way past a wimpy five stars—you deserve ten or more." With a mischievous glint in his eye and a crooked smile, he added, "You'll understand we do need to sign it Mr. and Mrs. Smith."

Lily roared with laughter on her way to the kitchen for the mimosa makings and food.

JJ escorted Jo to the quiet table that overlooked the pretty garden through the painted window. The leaf and flower motif on the glass appeared plucked from the garden.

"I wonder who painted this," Jo said. "It's lovely. I bet it's cheerful when winter is having its way outdoors." She curled her fingers around his outstretched hand as if comparing the fit as well as the differences. "Honey, can we wander around the shops downtown and take it easy today? I'm certain you want to be at LouEllen's hosted podcast tomorrow because I do, too. But the shops in the town square are calling to me to find gifts for friends. I thought I saw a park too, where we might picnic."

JJ gently squeezed her hand and gazed into her eyes, straight to her soul. "I'm sorry our escape has gotten away from us. I've been distracted helping these folks with real-time digital damage control. I almost got into a shoving match yesterday with that creep on the video who I saw push another girl into his truck. I couldn't reach the truck before it roared out of the parking lot. Kids always seek you out. Did you see her?"

"No, I didn't. I was close to the doorway for the show and the crowd was thick."

"Jo. This vacation isn't as much fun as I'd planned, but I can't turn my back on them."

Jo's fingers stroked his hand. She gazed into his eyes. "JJ, you're my hero. I'm so proud that you won't let these people suffer. I hope you haven't thought I was complaining. I'm enjoying the puzzle pieces of this mystery. I mean, you can't tell me this isn't fun." He noted the sincerity of her tone.

JJ murmured as Lily burst through the doors. "My world would fall off its axis without a beautiful, insightful woman to fall in love with."

Lily set the tray on an adjacent table and picked up the glasses, filling each in turn. "Guess I'm right on time to interrupt love bird chatter like always." She set some plates between them. "Here are a few breakfast snacks to get you started. Toast one another, have a quick smooch, and enjoy the first course."

As if on cue, Jo and JJ raised their glasses, which sounded a pretty tone. "Here's to you, Lily. Best owner in town."

CHAPTER THIRTEEN

Now It's Personal

The morning sunlight spilled in through the windows on either side of the door and landed right in the foyer area where they were standing.

"Another spectacular breakfast, Lily," JJ said. "I feel stuffed to the gills."

Jo nodded. "I can't wait to be hungry again."

Lily beamed and gathered them into her arms. "Group hug, group hug." A round of chuckling filled the space.

"We're heading downtown to explore the square, shop by glorious shop," said Jo. "Are there any shouldn't-miss destinations? Our vacation is short, and I don't want regrets."

Lily furrowed her brow, concentrating. "You'll find several small boutiques of specialized merchandise worth your time. Fun places to explore. Plus, Bluff Bakery is a delight to smell and taste. You're coming to the afternoon podcast at LouEllen's, right?"

"Just because the chief wasn't interested in the threats and hacking attempts doesn't mean we're not." JJ gave her a reassuring hug. "We'll be there. Can you give us directions?"

Lily grabbed the pad and pen off the desk. She scribbled quickly and handed it over with a smirk. "There you go. I printed the directions for easier reading."

JJ's phone chirped as they reached the door of their rental vehicle. He scanned the text and returned the device to his pocket. JJ smiled at Jo's inquisitive look after he opened her door.

He entered the driver's side, fastened his safety belt, and started the car.

Jo snorted. "I get it. I'm Dr. Watson to the infamous Sherlock, but what was in the message that made you smile? Or is it too personal?"

JJ patted her arm and added an affectionate caress. "That was rude of me. Sorry. An associate of mine did some digging on the attorney representing Superior Import and Export. The company is a shell corporation registered in New Jersey, and the attorney, Wiley E. Purloin, is bogus. The Cheatham, Pilferus, and Pocketum Law Firm has no charter or record of practicing law in Texas."

Jo wrinkled her face, deep in thought for a moment. "When the clerk registered the transaction with the county records department, why wouldn't they make a note of a questionable or unverified law firm?"

"The only reason it wasn't flagged by the county or state is if the transaction wasn't recorded properly, if at all."

"Wow, JJ. You might be right about the clerk accepting a bribe to cover up a non-existent law firm. It would explain why she's so grumpy about showing the records. Are we going to the police with this new evidence?"

JJ smiled and caressed her cheek. "In this business of digital cat and mouse, you never alert your quarry about how close you are to uncovering their cheese. Besides, you met the chief. He won't be interested until we have something concrete. Proving a bribe would be tough for us to do. Anyway, let's park on the far side of the square, enjoy the sights, and prowl the stores Lily mentioned."

Jo brightened and kissed his cheek. "I'll take lots of pics, and we can get an ice cream mid-morning."

Jo flumped down next to JJ on a shaded bench seat, placing two small parcels by her feet. She laughed at siblings arguing over their ice cream. JJ turned to watch the folks in the square. One mom placed hands on her hips telling her husband it was his turn to corral their kids.

"Honey, you look tired," JJ said.

"Shopping is hard work when you hit every store in order. But we saw some interesting stuff. You got so animated in that antique store. Why the haggling on that funny typewriter?"

"That, my dear, looked like an enigma machine that the Germans used during World War II. The owner showed me the serial number and insisted it was the one captured from the Kreigsmarine U-Boat 505. It's the machine the German military used to encrypt communications to keep their battle plans from the Allies. At least it worked until the transmissions could be de-ciphered. The Allies broke the code. The rules of engagement for the German Navy contained an edict that if a U-boat had to surface because of attacking destroyers, they immediately threw the encryption machine and code books overboard to keep them from the hands of their enemy. The funny part is, that device initiated the computer age and is the pro-genitor to the smart devices everyone uses nowadays."

"I had no idea. How did you learn about this—studying in school? Or is it more because of your work?"

JJ hugged her close. "It's a long story. I'll tell you sometime. How about that ice cream you wanted?"

Pushing her hair back and refitting her ball cap, she looked into his eyes. "I thought you forgot."

"Not me. You guard this bench and our bags. I'll get us each a cone with two scoops of chocolate."

Jo admired the view as JJ headed across the street to Harry Thurgood's coffee shop since folks were walking out with cones scooped high in hand. "Please make mine vanilla and only a single scoop."

JJ glanced back with a wave and entered the crowded store. People in line were friendly and polite, but slow. A pregnant woman in front of him had two indecisive toddlers. "Ma'am, would it help if I lifted your children up to see the ice cream? I know it helped me decide when I was little."

She looked relieved. "Thank you. The doctor doesn't want me lifting the twins at this point. I only have a few weeks to go."

"No problem. Who's first?"

"Jenny, please."

He hoisted the curly top who grinned at being up high. She pointed to her favorite in the display case and said, "Mama, may I have the pink?"

Mama nodded and ordered a small peppermint cone.

JJ set down the child and picked up her brother. The young boy looked him in the eyes and patted his cheek. "I'm James." After a fast look into the case, he added, "Mama, I want the green one, please."

Mama ordered a pistachio for James and a scoop of coffee ice cream for herself.

"Ma'am let me pay for that for you. My pleasure."

"Thanks for your help." She smiled. "You're the young man staying at Flower with that pretty lady, right?"

"I am. Name's JJ."

"You're nice like everyone says. I'm Claire. Have a great day, JJ."

JJ placed his order which was quickly filled. He hurried outside and across the street, only to discover the packages but no Jo. He sat licking his cone, suspecting she ran into a nearby store and would return soon. No one was on the street. *I need to remind her not to leave bags on a bench, even in a small town with friendly people.*

He finished his cone and tried to keep hers in the shade, only to see the white rivers of cream streaming down the shell and puddling on the street. He was about to lick it dry, when a woman's yelp came from the direction of the courthouse. He scanned the area feeling his heart beginning to pound. JJ heard a thud and cry from the alleyway on this side of the building. Worried, he jumped up, tossed Jo's cone into the nearby trashcan, and sprinted in the direction of the sounds. He turned into the side street and spotted Jo in a heap on the ground.

Praying she was alive, JJ knelt beside her, relieved to see the rise and fall of her chest even though her eyes were closed. Gently, he rolled her over, noticing her ballcap was under her. He was careful not to pick her up until he determined her injuries. Jo's eyes fluttered, and she tried to speak, but only moaned.

"Jo, can you hear me and open your eyes, honey?" He felt her limbs but saw no scrapes or abrasions.

Jo opened her eyes and tried to concentrate on his face.

JJ's heart pumped like a jackhammer. "Are you with me, sweetheart? Please say something."

She focused. "Oh, JJ. I'm sorry."

He stroked her forehead and her cheeks. "It's okay. We'll fix it. What happened?"

"I saw them," she groaned. "Two young girls wandered up. I recognized one from the first podcast at Flower. I tried speaking to them in Spanish, but they kept looking around the empty street, not responding. The one girl made the hand sign for help, and I returned it. That's when I noticed the matching Band-Aids on their hands. I thought perhaps they covered a chip implant, so I showed them my scar from where I cut mine out. They paled and started to run. I called out and pleaded for them to stop. I chased them down this alley, then something hit me from behind. Everything went black."

She tried to sit up, her hand reaching to the back of her head. JJ assisted. "Ouch."

JJ held her down and looked at the back of her head. "Jo, it's a bad cut but not bleeding like crazy. I don't like that you passed out. Do you think you can stand, or would you prefer I carry you?" Determined, he reached out for her hand.

"I think I can walk if you help me up." She stood with assistance and leaned against him.

"Maybe I should carry you."

She shook her head slowly and winced a bit. "I'm fine. Let's go slow."

JJ reached around her waist providing additional support. He looked in the alley—it was empty, but it felt like someone watched them. "Let's get you back to Flower and evaluate the wound before we head to the hospital."

"No hospital. It's not that bad. I'm not dizzy."

JJ leaned down and picked up her ballcap, finding a folded piece of paper underneath. He read it aloud. "This is your only warning. Back off. Leave now."

"JJ, I don't like this threat. It makes me mad."

JJ senses his eyes filling with tears and anger like a fire in his gut refusing to burn out, as he placed her hat carefully on her head. "I want you safe, sweetheart, but I need to stay and fight. They made it personal. And we have legit evidence to take to Tommy later."

CHAPTER FOURTEEN

Count Me In

Lily fussed and bustled like a mama cat cleaning her kits. "There, child, this cold compress will reduce the swelling. I don't think you need stitches, it's not that deep, thank God." She handed Jo a glass of water and a pill. "This Ibuprofen should reduce the ringing in your head. Just rest for a bit."

"But the podcast is soon. I want to go with JJ to help if there's another issue. Please let me up. You said I don't need stitches so it can't be that bad."

Lily shot a glance at JJ. He shook his head dismissively. "It's okay, Lily. There's no arguing with her when she puts her mind to something. It's one of my favorite qualities of hers. Plus, she's one tough lady."

Lily's face contorted into annoyance and her lips thinned. "What's that supposed to mean? She seems a perfect match for your obstinate makeup, Mr. Do-Good, computer nerd."

"Oh good. You do understand, Lily."

Lily grinned and closed the door as she left.

JJ turned and faced his love. "Jo, get some rest. I'll take you with me to the show…under protest. I don't want you at risk of being conked again."

Jo studied him with a slight frown before her smile blossomed and eyes danced. "JJ, what if the girls were told to get me to follow them? The girl looked around quickly before she flashed the help sign. Looking back, it could have been an apology. This sort of training to do as told might get her food, extra clothes, or even a kind word. They were both thin. This man could be training and rewarding their behaviors. I'm right about them being captives. And I don't think you want me here away from your protection while you go with Lily. Plus, you'd be sad, thinking about me sulking alone in this room."

JJ let out an exasperated sigh and kissed Jo's cheek. "No wonder males are outclassed by their females. Let's go find Lily."

Lily laughed when they reached her downstairs and JJ related their discussion. "That's what we like. Men that do everything we want."

"Lily," asked JJ, "LouEllen's lounge doesn't have a lot of window space for folks to watch from outside, right? That suggests streaming media will likely be their best viewing."

Lily nodded. "Yep. LouEllen's been promoting heavy for this edition of the podcast."

"Jo, I need to be inside for security support," JJ mused. "Can you meander with the spectators? Don't take off, just capture photos. Tell folks it's for social media posting. Maybe do a couple of candid videos asking their impression of the show."

"Okay. That's a great idea. Maybe I'll get a picture of the girls and we'll have more evidence."

JJ smiled at her quick grasp of the possibilities. "Let me have your phone. I'm going to load a modest data gathering program to help test your theory."

"What do I do with it, JJ?"

"Honey, the program will do the work. You smile, be engaging, and let the technology hunt for you."

Jo scrunched her nose. "I get it, just modeling again."

"You're not often wrong, sweetheart. With this program you're hunting for kids with chips in their hands, or elsewhere. Near field communications of an insert will cause the app to chime or alert. If that occurs, you take a photo. Use your magical smile to make it casual and not intrusive. These thugs don't like contact and now they know you, so be discreet."

Jo clapped her hands together and got up to do a happy dance. "I get to be a secret agent. Got it." She went back to their room to change clothes and replaced her hat with a wider brimmed one that matched.

"Team, listen up," Mary Lou commanded. "We're live in five."

Caroline and Valerie complained in unison, "Wait! What? Look at the screens. Tell me were not broadcasting this naked orgy. Ugh, how disgusting!"

JJ bolted into action, his fingers racing across the keyboard of his laptop. "On it." Anxious minutes ticked by marked with non-stop tapping of the keys. "I see what they're doing. They replaced your transmitting server with theirs. That's how they're controlling the streaming of those vulgar images. A little digital hocus-pocus pushes it back on them." More typing. "Boom."

Five minutes passed, and LouEllen griped, "We're supposed to live talk about the threats to Magnolia Bluff, but all I see is this filth. I don't want my branding torched by these images. We're not a pornographic toy store!"

Still working, JJ placated, "Keep at it, ladies. I'm returning the favor to your attackers. I need a few more minutes to age out the internal references, addresses, and… Voila. The tables are turned."

Valerie was the first to cheer when her screen repainted. "Whoop! JJ the magician pulled our bacon out of the fire again."

"You can fawn over our digital hero later," Mary Lou stated. "We have a show to stream." Before they went live, she mouthed a silent *thank you* to JJ.

JJ chuckled, relaxing a bit upon fixing the issue in time. He heard some footsteps and angry words he couldn't make out from Madison. He straightened in response to Jo dashing into the lounge waving her cellphone.

CHAPTER FIFTEEN

The Tail of the Trail

Jo rushed over to JJ and dragged him to a side room. She nearly jammed her phone up his nose, she was so excited. "JJ, you gotta look."

"Honey, let me hold it. Your hand is shaking so badly I can't see what you're trying to show me."

"Sorry, I got scared. I spotted the same girls again with that guy who spoke to you when we were riding the horses. It looked like something was wrong because he held them by the scruff of their neck like a mama cat does with kittens. His face was contorted then he set them down talking and pointed like he's teaching them some sort of skill. I did like you said and snapped pics. He noticed and rushed me trying to grab my phone."

Just then a familiar voice stated, "I've seen him before. He pops up often where he shouldn't be."

Jo released a deep breath.

"Madison, thanks for joining our little party," JJ said.

"The reason I'm in town is to tell Tommy I've been getting reports of gun shots coming from that property," she offered. "The callers said they thought someone was hunting out of season. I spoke to the feedlot folks in town. Owner of the F-250 you described before has been buying bagged deer corn by the score.

His temporary plates aren't mapping to any database. I've tried to catch him in town to talk, but he ducks out each time I'm here."

"Why can't you just drive in and ask to talk?" JJ asked.

Madison smirked. "My daddy was a Texas Ranger. He warned me to never go in alone unless it's to the pot in your own house."

JJ chortled. "Sounds like your parental advice matched mine. How about we go in together? I'm good in a fight unless I'm sparring with my twin. Then half the time I wonder how I missed her side kick and landed on my back."

"I'm coming, too," asserted Jo.

"Jo, I'm not letting you out of my sight. Madison, I need a favor. As the local game warden, I expect you may have some wireless remotes that can take infrared photos of animal movement."

Madison cocked her head to one side and nodded. "Yes, my department has some."

"Can we use them for this exercise?"

Madison shrugged. "Sure, just so long as you know how to deploy them with the guard dogs inside the compound. I've met this weasel once, and he's not trustworthy. Getting on the property is one thing. Exiting the vehicle safely is quite another. I don't do dogs. I had a poor experience with some poachers who didn't want to give up their illegal kill. Their dogs were even more determined."

"No problem," he empathized. "We'll go with a discreet deployment around the front of the perimeter, so we can capture comings and goings. Not close enough to be spotted. Let's meet around dusk at Flower."

Madison nodded and left.

Jo and JJ held hands as they returned to their posts, watching until the show wrapped up with no more issues.

"Jo, if I'm right, we'll spot more than just critters on the cameras."

She smiled and added a hug. "Let's say bye to the podcasters and go back to change for dinner. I can't wait for Lily's special tonight. I hear beef empanadas and homemade guacamole are on the menu."

CHAPTER SIXTEEN

In the Cover of Night

Madison arrived at dusk and slid into the table at Flower. She felt tense not knowing the plan when she joined them for dessert and coffee before they took off. "JJ, are you comfortable with these devices? Most visitors to the Hill Country wouldn't know how to use this equipment."

JJ grinned. "I have a lot of experience from my family, some of whom served in the military. Jo travels a great deal and has taken advanced protection and security classes. You can't be too careful these days."

Jo showed Madison her tote with a laptop and extra batteries, along with a taser they purchased near the airport when they landed. JJ took the remote filming devices from Madison and inspected them, forming a mini deployment on the table.

"You have a great coverage design of the target area for the cameras, JJ. Nicely done. I'm a bit surprised."

"Madison, these'll work. I think we're set. Thank you."

"JJ, do you want me to store these in my tote, too?" asked Jo.

"No, I'll keep them in the separate tote so I can deploy them as needed. Madison, thanks for driving. I don't know the roads well enough to do this alone."

They drove for almost twenty minutes before Madison turned onto the rutted, dirt road.

"Thank you for coming along," she stated. "I know the SUV looks official with the lights and paint job, but back-up in case I need it is much appreciated. I'm a game warden, not technically law enforcement so you can ride along. When we get to the gate, let me— Hmm, look at that. The gate's open with no guards. Could be a trap."

"When we rode our horses," Jo recalled, "Mr. F-250 drove through then locked the gate after telling us to get lost."

"They must be having a party," JJ decided. "Let's be sociable and see if we can become gatecrashers. Let me plant two of the cameras on this side of the fence…assuming they aren't monitoring public land. Inside is likely different, so keep an eye out for red or blue dots of light."

Thinking aloud when JJ returned, Madison said, "If a bunch of folks are here, then it stands to reason the dogs are put up. Let's go and knock on the door. Visitors might get a nicer conversation with the local game warden and a couple of newspaper reporters."

JJ laughed. "You're quick, Madison. I like that. You do all the talking. We're here to follow up on a tip the paper received. Jo, we're role playing, but let's keep an eye out for curiosity seekers. No pictures without permission like a news team would do. This is a friendly call about gunshots being reported earlier today."

Madison slowed the SUV and parked close to the front door. "I was right, JJ. No loose dogs. Lots of very expensive vehicles. There's money in this multistory house with all the elaborate trimmings I suspect. Let's introduce ourselves."

A well-dressed cowboy of medium build, dark complexion with jet-black hair, answered the door. He stepped outside, closing off the view to inside. In a gruff and deep, Hispanic accented voice, the man greeted, "Ah, Game Warden Jackson, an unexpected pleasure. Who are your friends? What can I do for you?"

Madison stood almost at attention. He was polite, but she knew better than to trust a viper. "Mr. Hernandez, I recall we met in town a couple of months ago. I'm sorry to pull you away from your guests, but I've received complaints about gunfire from your property for the last few days around sundown. It's my job to investigate, as it sounds like off-season hunting. I need to ask what you or your hands are shooting."

Chuckling slightly, Mateo admitted, "I've an unanticipated problem. When I started this project, we installed eight-foot walls to keep the deer in so during the fall we could sell hunting leases to harvest the herd based on Texas's hunting laws. We've tried to keep them fed with corn, but the feral pigs on the property beat the deer to the corn. At two hundred-plus pounds, these beasts are formidable creatures. Trying to intercept the pigs poaching, one of my men was gored. He shot the animal. We determined the herd was extensive, and you know, Warden Jackson, they eat anything. I brought in hunters and offered a bounty for each varmint downed and removed. Since I don't believe there is a pig season, I didn't think anyone would complain, especially since the harvested hogs are donated to the county's hungry."

JJ stood quietly next to Madison who grinned in agreement. "I don't think we need bother you any further, sir. Feral pigs are a large nuisance here in central Texas. I hadn't heard of your donation, but it's appreciated. I trust you'll be serving some of the pork to your guests for dinner."

Mateo shrugged and cast his eyes down. "No. Since most of my attendees are Islamic, beef is the only grilled meat tonight."

"Attendees?" JJ commented. "Apologies if we interrupted a religious gathering. We assumed you were having a cookout for your friends. My name is JJ, Mr. Hernandez. This is Jo my co-reporter."

Mateo momentarily focused on Jo, took her hand, and brushed it with a kiss. "Charming, and so pretty."

Madison prayed that Jo would remain still and composed, even if she couldn't stop staring at the man.

Mateo said dismissively with a matching rise of his shoulders. "Sadly, I only cooked enough food for the invited guests. I'm unable to offer you to join. I hope you understand."

"Yes, of course," replied Madison. "I've kept you long enough. Return to your guests and enjoy your evening."

"Mr. Hernandez," JJ asked, "is this a religious event, or for guests from your far-flung import/export business, like for employee team building?"

Mateo's eyes darted up and down JJ in assessment. "You could put it that way. Our properties in town are a bit too confining and there is a lack of parking spaces. Good day, all. Warden Jackson, please close the gate on your way out, if you don't mind."

They walked toward the SUV and heard the door close. Madison added, "There's that 'git off my property', I expected, just stated nicer."

"Ladies," JJ deftly whispered, "my fake stumble is up next so I can plant two more cams. Argh"

Jo and Madison gasped and positioned themselves to shield JJ's crab-crawling activity. He followed the design and planted the cameras in convenient ground cover, then bounded up dusting himself off. Madison watched him deftly link the units to the mobile app and confirm their operation. Madison relaxed a bit that no one came outside. "Any cameras they have must be turned off or not monitored. Let's go, JJ."

Jo tugged Madison's arm and motioned. Madison spotted two small figures holding to the shadows sneaking away parallel to the ranch house. She opened the rear side door and, using a low bird whistle, got their attention and motioned them over.

Madison traced their movements from tree to bush to the open door. Madison and JJ sat in front. Jo was in the back with the hitchhikers. She was grateful Mateo did not open the door or question their delay in leaving.

Madison drove through the gate and several miles down the road before pulling over into a secluded turnout.

Jo, noting their darker skin tone and nearly black hair suspected they were Hispanic. She tried to get the hitchhikers to engage in friendly chatter in Spanish. "Are you girls going someplace special? We can drop you."

"No, I'm Camila and she's Renata." The girls held one another's hand, saying nothing more.

"You must have worked hard today; your clothes show a few stains. What sort of work do you do?"

One replied, "We're housekeepers."

"Oh, do we need to take you back to your jobs."

The girl closest opened her eyes wide, showing fear. Then she shook her head.

Jo noted their thinness, possibly malnutrition, with bony elbows, hollow cheeks, loose clothes, and dull hair. "Are you hungry? We could help you get food."

They looked at Jo and nodded, spewing a rapid exchange.

"Jo, what have you learned?" JJ asked after a pause.

"The girls are called Camila and Renata. They stay at the Hernandez compound usually behind locked doors but get to come to town to steal information. They're afraid, and were trying to escape."

"Hi, girls," Madison interjected. "Nice to meet you. Do you have family? I can take you there if you tell me the directions."

"Madison," Jo interrupted, "I don't believe they have family here. They are both sporting filthy Band-Aids on the backs of their hands. JJ, can we check for chips later? Mostly they're scared, hungry, and in need of a bath and clean clothes."

JJ nodded. "We can't take them back to Flower. Lily would bombard them with questions. Madison, can you recommend any options?"

"I could call it into Child Protective Services, but it's too late. How about we head over to my house? I live alone and have extra bedrooms."

The girls both delivered a burst of Spanish to Jo then huddled in the corner of the backseat by the door.

"These girls can't go to the authorities," Jo said. "They think they'd be recaptured. They don't trust police, but I don't know why. Both are terrified. Their trust in us is like a tightrope made of hair. Let's go to Madison's and find out what we can."

"Madison," JJ asked, "can you take me to my car and then allow us to stay with you? We can reassess in the morning."

"Sure, JJ. You're both welcome, as are the girls. Lily would raise a cry for help if you didn't both sleep at the B and B, so call her and let her know after we grab your car. You can follow me to my place. We can set up the capture for the monitoring devices you planted."

"Sounds good. Will that work, Jo?"

"Perfect."

Jo confided to the girls, "*Todos vamos a Madison's a comer y descansar. Estara bien.*"

Both girls nodded with guarded smiles.

CHAPTER SEVENTEEN

Earn Your Pay

Mateo's eyes focused fiercely on the horizon. He felt the tension from the sensation of his jaw flexing and teeth grinding. Tired of listening to excuses, he bellowed, "Your talented hackers can't stop the podcasters? Our contract didn't contain a *can't* clause. My brother said you're the best… You've touted taking global organizations and governments to a standstill. You said you've defeated armies of security staffs. But one hotshot hacker beats you? Perhaps you can recommend a professional disrupter."

He paced a few steps, stopped, and moved back, but kept out of hearing range of his guests. "Your behavior is like a kindergarten squad rather than a Darknet threat who's supposed to impair digital activity…I don't give a crap how many other people you've helped. I want results to stop these *abuelas mayores* from one simple podcast from a podunk town in Texas… These people focus on ranching, farming, and Friday night beer drinking. Nothing remarkable outside of a town square with a clocktower … Enough. I don't want to hear any more excuses. I want today's event to fail and NOT go on air…"

Mateo paced in the other direction. He stopped before a wide window. All that was visible this time of night were lights of the town. "What is your plan to derail the podcast?... Really? That sounds like it has teeth and will gain the upper hand at last. I want to see them cry with this flagrant failure. Disappointing me is NOT an option…Pay you?"

Mateo threw back his head and laughed. He switched the phone from one hand to the other.

"Big demand from a group that hasn't delivered. You've got the down payment. Be happy I'm not demanding a refund. You're beginning to cost me…" Mateo shook his head. "Payment based on delivery. That's how I run my business. My supply meets the demand for my clients…Don't fail. You will regret the payback."

Mateo mashed the dial pad of his smart phone again for another number. When the call connected, he demanded, "Where are we with interrupting their tech support? He's not taking your hints. I've met him; he thinks he's tough shit…The direct approach, huh? Why didn't you do this earlier?…" He shook his head as he felt a headache beginning from this discussion. "We have an agreement. You help divert the podcasters' attention from me and my business in exchange for insurance coverage…Stop whining. They're fine today, even free to move around and do their chores. No harm will come to them because you're going to deliver."

Again, he began pacing. "I'm working on persuading the chief to protect my interests. He can't keep ignoring me. He doesn't have enough power not to…Any news on my missing inventory? The purchasers will be here in two days to complete the transaction. These are not the kind of buyers to disappoint… Yes, we scoured our property from the walls in. Nothing pinged. They're fast as the deer and quieter than grass growing…What?... Or someone gave them a lift. Dammit! The game warden and the two phony reporters."

Mateo nearly heaved the phone through the window. "Can you investigate it?…I know it's risky, but you can be careful. I can't have Warden Jackson turning them over to Child Protective Services when I have buyers that picked in advance…All right, have my three associates conduct a hit. Make it a memorable lesson. I need him neutralized. Set it up."

CHAPTER EIGHTEEN

Social Engagements

Tommy watched the video feed showing Mateo square his shoulders, his tee-shirt emphasizing his barrel chest. His damp black hair was disheveled when he entered the office. "Chief Jager, Officer Mendoza said you asked me to visit. I was picking up supplies, so now was good for me."

Tommy steeled his features as he recognized the visitor. "Gloria, why don't you go take a walk around the square and check on folks."

Gloria looked between the two men and nodded. Tommy noticed the appraising glance Hernandez made as he half smiled when she walked by him.

"Mr. Hernandez, thanks for stopping in. Please have a seat." Mateo ignored the extended hand. Tommy indicated the chair on the other side of his desk. "I wanted a word with you regarding some citizens' concerns."

Unable to hide his annoyance, Mateo stated, "Your gossipy town criers are still hounding me for details. Their streaming allegations are borderline libel. Now you want to bring up citizen concerns. What about me? I received an unannounced visit from your game warden who said people are complaining about gunshots they think are coming from my property. It's my property."

Tommy looked the man straight in the eye. "I hadn't heard about that. I'll follow up. The podcast group is getting threatening emails, computer hacks with ransomware payloads, not to mention a guest of Flower got hit on the head hard enough to make her unconscious for several minutes. Since the topic is your compound, I wanted to let you know. It might go a long way if you would just meet your neighbors."

"I'm supposed to let these women cast aspersions on me with no response?" Mateo growled. "I don't retreat from insults, especially from women. Women have only one purpose, and none of those bitches are worth a second look. My ranch isn't any of your town's concern. I pay my taxes. Why aren't you stopping them?"

"They're focused on community involvement. With some of the border issues over illegal immigrants, they feel it's their civic duty to make certain neighbors know one another. But… There must be a way we can make this a win-win."

"You're a wuss," Mateo sneered. "Are you sweet on one of them gals? I have rights to privacy, which I reinforced with a wall surrounding my spread. A few of my workers come to town to eat or buy supplies. That's all the community contribution needed. If you can't do your job and get them off their bandwagon, I have lawyers on my staff who can add a firm hand."

Unimpressed, Chief Jager snapped, "Then explain it to the podcasters on open mic. You can easily remedy this by speaking to them."

They glared at one another like boxers circling in a ring.

"Think about it, Mr. Hernandez. As a side note, do you have any high school age students who need enrollment? I'm asking as a matter of friendly courtesy."

"No, Chief. None of my workers have children of any age. I have a couple of women working on the ranch as cooks and cleaners. They sometimes come into town for errands."

Tommy stood. "Good to know. In case that changes while you live here, we do have a good set of schools. Thank you for coming in, Mr. Hernandez."

"Keep those women off my back."

"Have a nice day and make nice with the town. It'll go a long way."

Jo and JJ woke in each other's arms with the sun starting to chase away the darkness. "Good morning, sweet," JJ whispered with a tender kiss to his love.

"I'm still tired after helping Madison with the girls. Their hair hadn't had a good combing in some time. I think they're both pretty and quite intelligent."

"And they know how to eat. They ate twice as much as me. Renata wants to remove the chip, but she's scared. I'm certain she'll decide to have it out when she's ready. I won't press her. I'll see if I can test some of its capabilities this morning. It's a tracking device, but the app doing the searching needs to be within proximity—like maybe half a mile at the most—to get a reading. Any idea why Camila refused to let us check her?"

"She's been captive longer than Renata and seems more resigned to her fate. If she provides value at the compound, she avoids the alternative of being sold to a pimp or worse. Horrific options for a girl not yet sixteen. It's going to take a lot of trust and conversations to get all the information from either of them. The only reason they're speaking to me is because I related my imprisonment in Brazil."

"Jo, it's very brave of you to tell them your story and befriend these girls. You were right, honey. I'm sorry it took me a while to get on board."

"I think Madison will help protect them. I asked her last night if they could remain here for a few days before she called social services. Her daddy's a retired Texas Ranger so her upbringing is by the book, but she agreed."

"That's good to hear. I want to do research on the chip. And then there is the podcast this evening at the bar. Did you want to go or stay here with the girls?"

"Honestly, JJ, I think I'm more useful here, but I'd like to see the end of the show. The podcasters have tonight and then another show on Sunday, right?"

"That's what Lily said. I hope to have this resolved before then and give Chief Tommy enough evidence to get convinced. I still think he should be acting on what we've provided, but Texas is unique and has its own rules."

"Do you think Mateo is dirty?"

"I do. He seems to have an inside track, but I don't think Tommy is it, or any of the podcasters. At some point, somebody will make a mistake. I just wish it would happen soon."

"Me too. Let's get up and help Madison prepare breakfast, JJ."

CHAPTER NINETEEN

Last Call Cantina

Mary Lou was worried about the show tonight resonating with the citizens. "Ladies, slow down on the chips, salsa, guac, and tequila shots!" Mary Lou admonished. "We're here to do a podcast at the Last Call Cantina, not to power down their crowd pleasers. You act like you haven't eaten in days."

Jose laughed, his mustache wiggling. With his slight accent he soothed, "Chica, Mary Lou, it's fine. Don't worry. I won't set anymore out until around four, with the podcast starting at five." He turned to Lily. "Lily, I'm glad you brought the snacks. One of these days you'll agree to that catering contract I keep pushing to you. Your salsa is better than my mama's, but don't tell her."

Mini, his wife of twenty years, playfully punched his shoulder. "But not better than mine, right?"

He turned and picked her up and kissed her. "Never. Ladies, let me know if you need anything to finish setting up." Then, wagging his finger at them, he added, "No more shots until the show finishes. I know everyone will enjoy celebrating our fifteenth year in Magnolia Bluff. This kickoff with your podcast, plus our new Friday night musical talent contest, will keep us strong for another fifteen, right Mini?"

"*Sí*, Jose."

LouEllen, Valerie, and Caroline defiantly slammed back their last shots, then wiped the excess from fingers and mouths before taking up their positions.

Mary Lou glared at them then turned to JJ. "JJ, even though Jo will join us later, are you ready to keep us on the air? I don't know what they'll try this time."

"Yes, ma'am," he replied, focused on the latest guest to enter the bar. "Good day, Mr. Hernandez. Are you here for the celebration event, or do you have hidden musical talents for the contest later?"

Mary Lou felt her shoulders tighten, and frowned. She trusted JJ to avoid making things worse.

Mateo shook his head. "Oh, you're a reporter and you help this group of busybodies?"

JJ grinned. "I provide a bit of tech support, sir."

Mateo surveyed the podcasters like a shark circling its prey. His chest puffed out as he narrowed his eyes and smugly commented, "I thought I'd witness the podcast character assassination show."

Mary Lou jeered, "Glad to see you in the light, Mr. Hernandez. I can get you copies of the past shows, if you want."

"No need. My attorney handles assembling documentation for my lawsuits."

"Nice to see you here, Mr. Hernandez," Valerie innocently commented. "We'd love to interview you and let the town hear your responses. You won't pass up the opportunity to defend your actions on open mic, will you?"

Mateo delivered a dismissive look as he clucked his tongue. "Me, talk with the podcast pornographers? You overestimate your charm." He turned and faced the barkeep. "I'd like a double shot of Patrón, if you offer the good stuff."

Jose set down a shot glass and poured a generous double. "I cater to all my customers, señor, even those not friendly with the community."

LouEllen rocked back in her chair and mumbled, "Podcast pornographers, indeed. Has a catchy rhythm, don't you think? Wonder if it's a patented on-air title."

Mateo filled a small plate with the free munchies, and grabbed his glass, sauntering to the corner table.

The place filled up quickly with friendly faces greeting one another. Everyone snagged their drinks and snacks as they crowded into the space. Mini took orders and filled requests with seasoned efficiency.

As the clock tower struck five, Mary Lou issued orders, their standard intro music filled the air. Father Gorman stepped up to the mic. Mary chuckled as he grinned at some of the new faces.

"Nice to see y'all here, Gorman opened. "Hope to see you again Sunday morning. Ladies and gentlemen, thank you for joining today's Magnolia Bluff podcast. During today's discussion, our host may open it up for questions and comments. Our sponsor today is Jose Chavarria, co-owner with his wife Mini, of Last Call Cantina. We're celebrating their fifteenth anniversary of this fine establishment. Tonight's special is two-fer-one shots and free entry to the Best Musician contest, which will become a Friday regular. Now here's What's Happening in Magnolia Bluff."

The lights went out. A collective gasp filled the air.

Mary Lou hollered, "Jose, didn't you pay the electricity bill?"

"Lights are out for the whole block, Mary Lou, so it's not just here," Carolyn remarked from the exit door.

Several of the attendees lit the flashlights on their cell phones. The podcasters pointed their lights toward JJ. He shrugged and put his hands up fatalistically. "Ladies, computer equipment and telecommunications work if you have electricity. I can cure most problems except that."

"Folks, stay in your seats," Jose said. "We might get power back in a few minutes. Mini, pass around the snacks. I'll set up a round of drinks."

A few of the patrons cheered, "Thanks, Jose."

Mateo got up from his spot in the back and grinned. Meandering around the tables catching subdued conversations here and there, he stopped at the podcasters' table. His face shadowed in the half-light, showed a slight smile though he glared at the silent hens. "I hate eating in the dark, but at least you've stopped clucking." He whistled *Vaya con Dios* to the door and into the night.

JJ opened the app on his cellphone and tethered his laptop. He connected to the internet and identified the local city power station. "Who can I talk to at the power station? I need a name, please. And someone's phone."

Caroline dialed the number and handed JJ her phone. "Ask for Frank."

The friendly voice of a person not a machine, recited her standard message. "We're aware of the outage and are doing everything—"

"Let me talk to Frank," JJ interrupted. "Tell him I can fix his computer terminal problem. I just need him to grant me access via the internet...Yes, I know he is not supposed to do that...I'll hold, ma'am."

Jose's emergency battery backup lit two soft lights and kept his refrigeration system running. The light from a few of the cellphones, along with JJ's laptop screen, created a surrealistic interior to the bar with Mini serving customers and patting shoulders as she moved. The podcasters, uncertain of their fate, stared at JJ. Father Gorman sat on the side with his hands in prayer. Valerie snatched a few more munchies as Mini passed by.

JJ snapped to attention. "Yes, sir. We're without electricity at the Last Call Cantina along with every business in this block. I bet you're seeing a ransomware demand on your command terminal, preventing the system from restarting…No, sir, I'm not the hacker. My name is JJ Rodreguiz and I run a security company in Brazil. If you'll give me internet access and the IP address of the machine, I have tools to remove the beastie. With a little time, I think I can get the electricity back on."

LouEllen grabbed the phone. "Frank, it's me LouEllen. You're speaking to JJ. He's been helping us fight these cyberattacks. Please do what he asks. We think he can fix it." Tears formed in her eyes as she handed back the phone. "Do your magic, JJ."

JJ nodded as he listened. "Yes, sir, that's what I need…" He tapped the keyboard then nodded. "Frank, I'm in and taking control of the device. You can watch the cleaning protocol."

Guests in the bar held their breath. Jose stopped pouring. Mini, along with everyone else, stared at JJ. An eternity of minutes passed.

"There. Bang! You're dead," JJ exclaimed. "Frank, can you oblige us with…Perfect. Thank you."

Cheers erupted as the lights came up, and the wi-fi recycled and connected. The router began communicating with the hosting server.

He disconnected the call and handed it back to Caroline. "Show time, ladies."

They high fived one another, even Mary Lou. She felt relieved they'd won yet again.

CHAPTER TWENTY

Pleased to Beat You, Nacho

Gloria approached JJ while he wrapped up his gear to leave. "It seems half the podcast drama is about you working digital magic. Until you arrived, I thought the biggest crime around here was stealing donuts. People say the random cyber-attacks are trying to take the podcasters off the air, but you step in like a white knight and everything is wonderful. I am skeptical of fairy tale endings, but you seem sincere. Chief Tommy says it's all marketing or showmanship to get listeners to tune in and listen to their gripes. What do you think?"

He ruffled his hair in frustration. "I'm surprised at your interest when he barely gave us the time of day in his office. I'm happy to show you the threatening emails the podcasters received, the handwritten note I got, and of course my girlfriend Jo was hit on the head and knocked out." JJ unpacked his PC, booted it, and pulled up the evidence copies he'd saved. He handed the copies to her and opened the electronic samples of the emails.

Gloria's eyes widened while she looked at the information. She shook her head as if doubting the results. "You showed Tommy these threats?"

"I gave him copies," JJ groused. "My itemization was discounted. It seems from the way your jaw muscles are flexing that he didn't share the evidence with you. Nope. He's not interested, and even indicated you had a heavy workload.

Gloria protested, "There're many who still believe women should not be in law enforcement. Too delicate or some such nonsense. My dad wanted me to study criminal justice. I just wanted to get the bad guys like in the stories that CW Hawes and the rest of the Underground Authors write. Funny how things turn out. I've not been on Tommy's team that long, so I'm relegated to looking for a donut thief rather than tracking down death threats to our citizens." She wrung her hands. "That's not the way I want to serve and protect. I'd like to help with your case. Can you show me everything you've found so far? Something seems off."

"I agree. Not certain why Chief Tommy is ignoring the ladies' requests. If you can help, I'd appreciate it. I don't know all the local laws, but I do know technology."

"I heard Madison went to see Mateo and brought along you and Jo. You wanna tell me how that went?"

JJ pursed his lips and cocked his head to one side. "Jo and I have a theory, but we need to gather more proof for the chief. Mateo's compound is hiding something. I just don't know how big that is."

Gloria smirked. "Let's not burden the chief with too many details until, as you say, there's proof. He's busy and sorts through lots of issues. I hate seeing him fret over an investigation when I can help. I am kinda stalled on my donut case unless we get another occurrence."

"I love the support of you and the other folks in town." JJ grinned. "I'll take my gear back to Flower. We can get together and discuss what we've uncovered along with next steps. Heck,

I'd like to talk it out with you and show you everything we put together."

"Sounds like a great plan." Her eyes taking a top-down inventory, she added, "Do you have a brother somewhere you could introduce me to?"

JJ laughed. "No."

JJ called to Jose and waved as he exited the bar. The parking lot was dimly lit, and few cars remained. Before he reached his rental, three men encircled him. All three were dark skinned, black haired, and catcalling to him in Spanish. He recognized the F-250 driver but couldn't peg the other two.

"I told you, gringo, stay out of this mess. Now you'll pay."

"I'm on vacation and I'm growing fond of this town. I like Flower. Food's good." JJ realized the two others were the grumpy breakfast guys that had left the dining room in a huff. He considered they ate at Flower to hear gossip. Unable to take his eyes off the approaching thugs to unlock his rental, he heaved his computer bag under the car, while he dodged the wild punch from the first assailant. Realizing he was the target, not his laptop, he backed into a familiar fighting stance, grateful and for his martial arts training.

F-250 had a knife he shifted from hand to hand. His taunting comments were unintelligible. The third man used an axe handle like a baseball bat. The brass knuckles of the first guy missed their target. They circled but appeared unorganized. JJ kept moving.

He taunted, "Hey, Nacho. Bet your boss is mad at the failed cyberattacks. Ha! Mateo must be pissed at me closing in on his operation. He's sending you to hurt me."

"My name's not Nacho, gringo," F-250 growled. "I plan to cut your fingers off after my boys make sure you walk with a limp for six months. You can use that keyboard with stubs."

The other two laughed and drew closer. Axe Handle was first up. He swung and missed. JJ turned at the last second and drove a powerful side kick into the man's ribs. The force of the hit sent the man into a parked car. His head ricocheted off the vehicle. He landed on the ground facedown.

"Nacho," teased JJ. "I'm saving you for last. Didn't *yo madre* teach you not to play with knives? You know you can cut yourself if you aren't careful. I bet you're never careful."

Banter distracted brass knuckle guy for a second too long. JJ extended his leg and spun. He timed his foot extension perfectly. His momentum caught the side of the thug's head. JJ landed on his toes, switched feet, and delivered a blow to the man's solar plexus. The whoosh of the man's exhale echoed in the empty parking lot. JJ danced away as man two crumpled into a heap on the asphalt.

Nacho glanced at his buddies on the ground. Useless. Fear flickered across his face as the lights of the lot crossed his eyes. His awkward movements assisted JJ in planning his next attack.

"What fingers were you planning to cut, Nacho?" JJ goaded. "Mine or yours? That heavy sweat beading on your face is running down your arm. Watch it, Nacho. Your knife will slip and slice you. You want me to drive it into you for safe keeping?"

Nacho loudly cursed and rushed JJ. He desperately slashed his knife side-to-side in wide arcs. JJ sidestepped the knife and caught the man under the chin with the edge of his practiced hand. The abrupt chop displaced Nacho's balance resulting in him propelling horizontally for seconds before JJ shoved him down on his back. The wind rushed from the man's lungs. JJ witnessed his eyes roll back in his head.

JJ spat. "Nacho, I bet you're the one who hit Jo on the head. No one messes with me or my family without payback." JJ delivered multiple sledgehammer-like blows to the man's ribs yielding a satisfying crack. JJ stood and looked at the unconscious man. "Someone told you to work me over. I've sparred with better fighters. Thanks for the workout, but I'm not-cho punching bag."

Gloria appeared, sidestepping the shadows. She clapped. "I admit, I'm impressed, JJ. With them out like Christmas, can you help me get them into the car for the ride to the station. Are they more of your evidence?"

JJ smiled and laughed. "Might be if you cuff 'em. Been standing there long?"

"For a little bit. You were doing fine. I spotted them lurking outside Last Call earlier. I thought they'd pull something but didn't expect they'd attack you. I woulda stepped in before letting you get hurt." She reached around for one set on cuffs. "By the way I timed your exercise. Congratulations, you beat the top police academy takedown score. You might consider a whole other career."

CHAPTER TWENTY-ONE

Friend or Foe

Jo experienced a kinship of sorts with these girls in learning more about their lives. Jo chatted away in Spanish with Camila and Renata while they ate an early dinner. They had gone to bed late and slept most of the day. Jo was delighted they trusted her enough to chat on any level. The details of life in the compound weren't a topic they explained.

When Jo inquired, they deflected or became silent and unwilling to share specific details. They were both pretty with smiles that could light up a room, but Jo felt they were under nourished. Their hair was a dull and nails worn. The stylish clothes Madison provided fit with room to expand. She laughed when they asked for seconds at dinner.

"I took two years of high school Spanish," Madison commented, "but all I can remember to say is *una cerveza, por favor.*" The girls giggled.

In Spanish, Jo commented, "Camila, Renata, please place your dishes into the sink and go wash your hands and faces. Ms. Madison put some fresh tee-shirts on your beds if you want to change."

The women move to sit in the den while the girls finished their chores. Jo studied Madison. "People tend to speak more freely in their native tongue. The girls do speak bit of English and have had a little education. They are scared they'll be dragged back to that place. Neither have parents living."

Madison appeared chagrined as she looked away. "I get it." Madison admitted. "When they're in protective custody, we can make certain they're guarded. You have a bond, so don't go far. I spoke to Gloria and gave her some details. She suggested we meet her later at the bar when the podcast is over."

Jo nodded. "She seemed nice when we met at the police station. I bet the girls will like her especially as she speaks Spanish fluently. Maybe Gloria can get them to share more about their situation inside the compound."

Madison looked off into the distance. "I wonder how many more of these young'uns there are. Not just in the compound either. We have too many illegal immigrants who enter without a plan or place to live. The stories you related reminded me that the human trafficking issues are pervasive. But it's bad here. My dad mentions it often and tries to lend aid when he can."

"I agree. The problem is widespread. Their chips, JJ discovered, are like ownership with numbered identity. These girls are property. Their owners have all the rights. They have no idea who they'll be slaves to when they're sold. It's awful. Tragic." Jo took a breath and blinked back tears. "I hope the show went well. I pray there were no incidents."

The girls entered, freshly scrubbed and wearing clean shirts.

Camila grinned. "Thank you, Señora Madison, for the outfits. They fit perfectly."

Renata nodded. "*Gracias*, Madison and Jo."

"You both look lovely," Madison exclaimed. "Remember, we're going to town to meet with Officer Mendoza, and she will make certain you are safe in protective services. The folks there will help get you where you can be cared for."

After a short ride, Madison eased her SUV into downtown. "Hmmm…appears like a little excitement occurred. Let's cruise by and find a good parking spot."

Madison parked in an end spot on the square and turned out her lights. "Jo, you and girls stay here until I see what's up." She stepped out of the vehicle and sauntered over to the scene.

JJ looked up. "Hey, Madison. Did you bring the evidence?" Madison smiled at Gloria.

"Loading up these unconscious bodies leaves you no room to take the girls with you, Gloria," JJ joked.

Recognizing JJ, Jo got out of the game warden's vehicle. She and the girls waited and stayed to the shadows, until Madison indicated the situation was under control. Gloria's face was caught in the headlights of a passing car. Camila froze. Renata followed suit. The girls grasped each other's hands, sinking back further into the darkness provided by the bushes.

Renata whispered to Camila in Spanish. After Renata turned to Jo. "Miss Jo, it's her. The one he bargains with when one of us is taken. You said you'd help us. She works for the devil Mateo."

Camila turned, ran silent as a cat. In moments the darkness swallowed her silhouette.

JJ strode toward Jo while Madison remained with Gloria assisting with the prisoners.

"JJ, Camila took off when she saw Gloria," Jo related. "Renata's terrified and claims the deputy works for Mateo. She told me he brokers people like chattel."

JJ ground his teeth and ran fingers through his hair. He shook his head. "What a mess. We nearly surrendered these girls to one of the players. Is Madison involved up to her ears, too?"

"I don't think so. We worked together to get the girls cleaned up, dressed, and fed at her place. She's been kind, except for insisting they need child protective services support, not ours. Their fear of Gloria runs deep. What're we gonna do?"

"Does Madison think Gloria's dirty?"

"Madison wasn't here when the girls spotted Gloria. Based on other conversations, she likes Gloria and has known her a long time. Like professional friends, I suspect."

"Okay, let me see what I can do. We need to let Madison know, but not here." JJ clucked his tongue. He worried that he'd placed the girls and Jo in danger. He sauntered back toward the officers thinking of a way out. "Ladies, since I filled up the squad car with three assailants, I think it best if we keep track of the girls a while longer. Jo has a good rapport with them and speaks their language."

Gloria raised an eyebrow. "I speak Spanish, too, JJ. They'd be fine with me. But I wouldn't want them to ride with these guys."

"Gloria," JJ asked, "do you need my help to get them to the jail? I'd hate to have them turn on you and escape before I can press charges."

Gloria shuffled her feet. "You want to press charges? You beat them badly. The one you tagged as Nacho needs stitches. I plan to take them to jail and get the doc to look at them for some first aid."

JJ narrowed his eyes at Gloria. "You think because I'm from out of town I wouldn't made a court appearance. I'll be here and want to see justice done. I don't want to inconvenience anyone here in Magnolia Bluff. But these guys should not be turned loose. I'll file charges."

Madison studied the exchange with a furrowed brow but kept quiet.

Gloria sucked in her breath and stood ramrod straight. "Guys like you tick me off. I know how to do my job. I'll take them in and lock 'em up for seventy-two hours. They may press charges against you."

"I can help you transport them."

"JJ, I don't need your help. Madison, bring those girls you mentioned in the morning for the CPS folks. I left a message after you told me the situation." Stomping away, she slammed the door of her patrol car.

JJ winked at Madison and whispered, "I have my rental car over there." Pointing, he added, "I put my computer under it. I'll retrieve it and take Jo and Renata back with me. Camilla took off when she saw Gloria. Both girls said she works for Mateo. I know she's your friend, but her behavior has been odd tonight, especially not breaking up my fight with those three, who I know work for Mateo. Join us at Flower while we talk to Lily. Please don't let her know where you're going or that anything's wrong."

Madison looked unconvinced. "Understood, but I don't like it."

CHAPTER TWENTY-TWO

Tell Me It Isn't So

Lily stared dumbfounded at one face then another as she absorbed the confusing revelation. Jo, Madison, and Renata remained silent while JJ explained the events of the evening and answered as much as they knew.

JJ outlined the plan. "Lily, we're gonna need another room to keep Renata hidden. Jo will stay with her while Madison and I search for Camila. This much we believe: these girls are being trafficked and will be sold as part of Mateo's operation. She, and others like her, are the reason your podcasters were targeted. Your constant questions were making the bad guys famous. Illegal operations depend on anonymity."

Lily's mouth moved but her complete astonishment prevented any words.

"The most important thing, Lily, is you can't tell anyone. If word gets back to Mateo, his henchmen will take them by whatever means necessary. You could be at risk if they find out. Please don't tell anyone."

Lily finally strained her neck in a slow roll then swallowed. "You're saying our podcast poked a bear who is running a human trafficking organization? Someone on the Magnolia Bluff police force could be involved? Really? How many tequila shots did you have at Jose's cantina? Are you hearing yourself? I've known these people all my life. Where's your proof?"

JJ calmly pulled out his smart phone and browsed through several pages of apps before launching one. He looked at Jo. "Please ask Renata to show us her chipped hand."

Jo nodded reassuringly as she translated to make certain the teen understood. Renata extended her trembling left hand palm-down. JJ held his phone over her bandage and pressed the start key. In seconds, an information record was displayed with the title *Inventory*. JJ showed the screen to Lily and paged through the data revealed from the chip.

Tears formed in Lily's eyes.

"Can you imagine an inventory is so large that you have your merchandise computerized to track it?" JJ continued, "This shows the background history, and who has put a bid on the targeted item like it shows here, amount offered or tendered, and expected close dates. There's enough money flowing in this business for law enforcement to end up on the payroll. I'm sorry but Renata and Camila both identified Gloria as a handler for Mateo. This is the evidence we need to give to Chief Tommy. Renata mustn't get discovered here."

With her eyes glistening, Jo held out her hand to show her chip scar to Lily. "This is not joke, Lily."

Lily sobbed, "This is terrible, just horrible! Chipped human beings processed like produce. We had no idea. None." After deep breaths, she exclaimed, "Oh my God, we were talking about ending the show. We can't now. Look what we found."

"You're right, Lily, don't end the show," Madison reinforced. "You ladies need to keep the pressure on from the podcasts while we finish gathering more evidence. But like JJ says, not a word to anyone about Renata."

"Madison's right, Lily," JJ said. "I fought three of his thugs after the bar podcast. This tells me they're desperate to get out of the limelight. Keep the pressure on. They're bound to make more mistakes trying to get everyone to give up the onslaught." He turned to Jo. "Jo, keep Renata safe while Madison and I look for Camila."

"I need to come, too. JJ, I know you speak Spanish, but Camila will talk to me. Madison knows the area, so it makes sense for her to drive. I'm the best to calm her when we find her."

Almost chuckling but still wiping the tears, Lily croaked, "She did it again, JJ. Her feminine logic pinned you. I'll put Renata in the room next to yours so Jo can shuttle back and forth. That room is under renovation and can't be rented to anyone. I'll make sure she's safe while you're gone." She faced Renata. "You'll stay with me while their gone, sweetie."

Renata looked to Jo who whispered something. Renata joined to Lily's side. "*Si.*"

Madison laughed at the sour look on JJ's face. "Right," he complained. "Which one of us is Dr. Watson, Ms. Sherlock?"

Jo delivered a quick peck on JJ's cheek. "Let me get Renata settled, then we can leave. Lily, she's probably hungry. Could you possibly—"

Lily smiled and marched towards the kitchen with Renata in tow.

CHAPTER TWENTY-THREE

Lost and Found

"Ladies, where do we start?" JJ asked. "If you were running from the devil, where would you go? What would you do to evade capture?"

Staring out the window of the game warden's cruiser, Jo reminisced, "I'd avoid human contact and stick to properties with lots of foliage. Move at pre-dawn or dusk. Avoid roads."

"Staying off the streets makes sense. Going cross-country is at least five miles. It means ranch houses or barns," Madison mused. "Around here they're not close together. Navigating fences could pose a problem without lighting. Livestock can be unpredictable. Homes are secluded with little or no lighting to navigate the fences. You'd have to have a direction in mind to get to your destination rather than travel in circles."

"Jo, did Camila talk about her home or family?" JJ asked. "Did she mention her likes or dislikes? We've no idea what she'd consider a safe place."

Jo turned and grinned. "Camila said she loved playing in water and missed her animals. Her family was poor, and her two brothers jobbed out to ranches. Neither girl revealed where they were from other than to say they became friends at the compound. I think they are ashamed their families didn't want them. She might have been sold because the family was poor. It's a sad culture that doesn't value females except as property. We have no way of knowing if she'd been sold before. I'm thankful she'd not using drugs."

Madison turned red as she insisted, "My daddy never treated me that way! He was supportive and encouraged me to always drive toward my dreams. Guys made fun of me for going into law enforcement, but some of them admitted they were impressed with my gumption. However, you may not be wrong, Jo. In some cases, it's true that the young men can work harder for a wage. Though out along the border further south, they bring in young men and women for resale…or worse." Madison took a deep breath "Based on what you learned, Jo, let's look toward the reservoir. At least she'd have fresh water. There are small semi-camping areas on the south side where someone might beg for food. Let's just hope she doesn't bump into the reservoir pole-fishing trash. Those folk practically live there year 'round. Let me do the talking."

JJ smiled. "If we don't get any leads on her, let's swing by Hank's place and ask him to keep a lookout. At this point I'd like to minimize what we say on the phone."

Two hours of searching and questioning turned up nothing. They returned to the cruiser. "I'm sorry, you guys," Madison conceded. "No luck tonight. No one's seen her. The couple in the camper hadn't seen anyone alone walking and the others were responsive to questions, so I doubt she was grabbed. Let's call it a night. We can try early. JJ, you need to be fresh for tomorrow's podcast. They're sure to be even more desperate to stop it now."

JJ smirked. "Agreed. Can we swing by Hank's and alert him, Madison? I think he'd help if we explained the situation."

"It's getting kind of late, but I don't think Hank will mind if we pester him. Don't laugh if they're in their jammies sipping whiskey on the porch."

"Maybe we shouldn't bother them tonight," Jo cautioned. "I'm not sure I could un-see the image."

JJ chortled. "Jo, I'm thinking the same thing."

Madison chuckled then laughed aloud with tears running down her cheeks. "Okay, I'll text him to save you from the vision. I'll get 'em to put on clothes before greeting us. They've got a ritual of taking their favorite beverage, then strolling to the reservoir au naturel for a sweetheart swim. I guess things at nineteen still work for fifty-plus."

Jo and JJ shared a look and grinned.

"Alright," Madison announced. "We're here. Let me go first to avoid messing with your delicate sensibilities." She disappeared inside and emerged moments later with Hank and Ann.

"Come on up here and sit, you two," Hank called.

When they were seated, Hank offered them a drink.

JJ related the situation. He noticed that Ann clutched her husband's hand a bit tighter than needed for a friendly conversation. Madison had stressed the need to keep the information close to the vest while avoiding their suspicions of Gloria.

JJ sensed an increased tension in the air. He watched their faces as he highlighted. "All we're asking is that you alert us if you see this girl. We're trying to help her, but when she got frightened, she took off like a rabbit into the dark."

Jo leaned toward JJ and whispered to him. He further assessed the situation with the looks between Ann and Hank. He shouted in Spanish, "Camila! We're here to help you. Don't keep running. We won't let them take you, honey."

Hank looked between the nighttime visitors. "Camila, come on out. I'll protect you. Ann will, too."

Camila squeezed out the screen door and drew up behind Hank and Ann. Ann raised a hand up to her shoulder, and Camila latched on with trembling fingers.

Hank patted it. "I heard the horses nickering and stomping in the barn. I worried maybe I'd left the door ajar, and a coyote or some other threat might be messing with them. I went to check on them and found her brushing Midnight. Poor thing was crying a river while she talked to him." Hank took a sip of his whiskey and continued, "She told us about the situation including the part about Gloria. I've known Gloria a while and I find it troubling that she's working with that scum. I learned to speak Spanish to work with my ranch and deal with the locals. Camila knows more English than she lets on but is more comfortable in her native language. I won't let you take her if she doesn't want to go. She doesn't need any more heartache."

Camila rushed around and knelt in front of Jo. She hugged Jo's knees and sobbed. Jo looked toward JJ for support.

"Camila's safe here," Madison commented. "Hank, if you're willing, can we bring Renata here so they can stay together? I know it's a lot to ask, but no one would suspect them being in your possession."

Jo embraced Camila. "I don't want to leave her. No offense, Hank, but we can take Camila back with us, then bring both girls back when things get sorted out."

Hank nodded but said nothing.

"Nobody can know where they are," JJ stated. "Mateo has snitches everywhere, I'm sure. Until the police are vetted, these girls are evidence, and at risk."

Madison nodded agreement. "The last time they were seen and acknowledged was in Jo's custody. Jo is typically with you. Parking them here, Jo, might be smarter. They'd be in a quasi-protective custody."

Jo turned to Camila. "Camila, would you feel safer here rather than going with us?"

Camila looked at Hank and Ann then back to Jo. "I miss Renata and I am glad she's with you—safe. I think she would be better here. We could even stay in the barn. But I'll do what you say, Miss Jo."

Jo's eyes filled with tears. "JJ, I'm torn. I want to help them so much."

Before he could respond, Madison grumbled, "I don't like this one bit. Both girls say Gloria's a bad apple, in on the game. Something's fishy. I can't put my finger on what. I'll find her in the morning and take her aside to ask."

JJ reached his arm over Jo's shoulders. "Jo, Camila is safe here. Let's get back to Flower and check on Renata. We'll bring her here in the morning. It'll give us time to do some additional research."

Jo looked up into his eyes and nodded. "Camila, you stay with Hank and Ann for now. No more running, okay? We'll help you. Enjoy the horses, *chica*." Jo embraced Ann and Hank in turn. "Please take care of her. JJ, let's get the rest of the needed evidence."

CHAPTER TWENTY-FOUR

Order to Go

"**W**hoa, Chief, I didn't expect you to answer," Madison admitted. "I was calling to talk to Gloria. Is she around?"

An annoyed Chief Tommy growled, "Nope. She's at the hospital being checked out after last night's fracas. It should have been a routine lock-up, but one got loose. The three of them worked her over. One of 'em took her service weapon, too."

Madison shouted, "Oh hell! Really? Those slimeballs got away. Damn!"

"Madison, tell me what you know. Gloria was barely conscious when I called the ambulance. Were you involved in the capture?"

"Chief, I arrived in the area when she was loading them up. I saw them in the dim light so not much to describe. The three guys attacked JJ. He is that computer nerd staying over at Flower helping the podcasters. He took on all three of these gang fighters and flattened them with his ninja/kung fu moves. Gloria was taking them to lockup and planned to meet JJ at your offices today to press formal charges."

"That kid again. He seems to either have a good guy streak or he's into something we don't want in our town."

"Tommy, that young man is onto something. He said he provided you some information and you ignored him. The podcast team is trying to get to the bottom of this community issue but keep getting whacked by a digital Armageddon. JJ's girlfriend was clunked on the head in an alley off the square. Now you have an officer down. Tommy, you need to talk to him again, only this time try listening."

"Don't lecture me on police business, young lady. But all right. Do me a favor and ask him to come in. And, Madison, can you lend a hand here at the station until Gloria gets back?"

Madison smirked. "Long as I don't have to chase after the donut bandit."

"Fine. Hey, bring me some of Harry's coffee from Really Good and some donuts with the little sprinkles on top."

Madison deadpanned, "I'll bring coffee from Lily's. That way I don't have to make two stops. Her pastries are better anyway."

It was just past dawn. Jo flinched at the rustling in the next room which startled JJ awake. "I'm gonna see how Renata's doing. I'll be right back."

JJ grumbled. "You've checked every hour since we turned in last night. Is she getting any sleep with all your concern, sweetheart?"

"Am I smothering? I'm just worried about her. I wish Camila were here with us. I want you to know how much…I mean, without you where would I be? Where would they be? Thank you, honey."

"Am I getting her food, or is Lily delivering up here? We don't want her downstairs on the off chance someone might see her."

"Yes, please, but later this morning. Go back to sleep."

Jo slipped back under the covers and nuzzled JJ. "Honey, I know we're here for us. This mess is a disruption, but I can't let it go. Thank you for understanding."

JJ kissed her and held her tight for a few moments. "I understand. We'll make up for it."

They drifted back into slumber, but Jo was jarred awake by tapping on the adjoining door. JJ sat up. Renata whispered through the partially open door, "Ms. Jo, is it too early to eat? I'm so hungry I can't sleep. I can get something from the cold box. I don't think Lily would mind; she's so sweet."

"No, but JJ might."

"Renata," JJ replied, "let me see what I can find for you. If Lily's awake, I'll ask for an early breakfast. I'd rather you stay in your room unless we're with you. I'll even help Lily make breakfast if I need to. Jo, you two get cleaned up, and please outline the boundaries while she's here. I'll be back."

JJ dressed and headed downstairs. He was greeted with the delightful smell of fresh brewing coffee. He spotted Lily cutting up veggies for breakfast, and dancing to the country channel softly playing. He chuckled, "Lily, thank the Maker, you're an early riser. I've got hungry ladies petitioning for breakfast. May I help in any way?"

"Good morning. You can. Pour coffee for you and Jo and git out of my kitchen workspace. I'll bring a tray shortly. By the way, Madison texted me she wants to speak to you. She's coming for coffee and sweet bread for Chief Tommy." Lily assembled a tray. "Here you go. Please let Jo know Madison's expected any minute."

CHAPTER TWENTY-FIVE

Less Talking, No Telling

Madison picked up JJ from Flower and drove to the court-house and parked.

"Madison, I don't want to mention the girls to the chief yet," JJ insisted. "I'd like more time to verify who's on which side, please."

"Agreed. I want to speak to Gloria in a little girl chat, too. I'm not going to mention this to Tommy at this point."

JJ carried the snacks into the station. He delivered them with a smile and inclined his head. "Morning, Chief Jager."

Tommy smirked. "You can call me Tommy. Thanks, Madison, for the coffee. Where's the cream and sugar?"

"Sorry, I picked up the order on my way out. I thought you wanted great taste." JJ sized up the man with the same intensity as he'd received. "You see, Lily's coffee is on par with the Brazilian coffees I drink. Outside of North America, everyone calls U.S. coffee dirty water."

JJ watched the near smile bloom on Tommy's face when he took a sip of the coffee.

"Heard you were stirring up trouble again yesterday after the podcast," Tommy said. "You wanna tell me about it?"

"Tommy, Last Call Cantina, along with shops along the block, had the power knocked out. It completely halted the podcast. Mateo left chuckling, which proves nothing, but the ladies asked him to speak on the podcast to the community. He refused. I called and was given access to the power station by the manager. He allowed me access to fix the malware attack that had seized the system. Odd how the malware only took out the block of businesses where the podcast was scheduled."

"You're right, that's odd, but circumstantial."

"Tommy, when everything was back online, I stayed in case of another assault. Fortunately, nothing else occurred. I packed up, was one of the last to leave. They were waiting for me near my rental, like vultures waiting for the final breath of life to exhale to start feasting. One carried a wooden axe handle, one had brass knuckles, and the third waved a knife. My father taught me the art of self-defense even if you are outnumbered."

"Did they say anything or just lash out?"

JJ chuckled. "Yeah, they called me a gringo. I'm half Hispanic, so it hurt my feelings. They told me to back off and leave town."

Madison chortled. "Remind me not to hurt your feelings. Tommy, when I drove up, the three were down and appeared out for the count."

"JJ, do you want to swear out a complaint?" Tommy asked. "It'll bring more weight to the discussion I plan with Mateo."

"They work for Mateo?" JJ sarcastically asked. "Small world."

Tommy ignored the comment and turned to Madison. "Can you get him the necessary paperwork and walk him through it to make certain the complaint is tight? JJ, is there any other evidence on this mess you want me to know about or to review?"

"I have some information. I promised you better stuff so let me finish my efforts. I don't want you having doubts. I do think the F-250 guy, who I named Nacho, is the one that hit my girl-friend. If I can prove it, we'll file an assault charge for that, too."

"JJ, I get you can take care of yourself. The ones close to you and friends you've made here could be at risk when someone doesn't get their way. Everyone around you needs to be vigilant."

Jo smiled at Renata as she brushed her hair. Jo sipped the coffee JJ had brought up before he left. Her face contorted. "Yuk, it's cold. Sweetie, I'm going downstairs to get fresh. I'll be right back. You stay here and finish getting dressed. Do you want anything more?"

"No, thank you, Jo. I'm feeling better than I have in days. Though next time, may I have a donut? I love 'em."

Jo was halfway downstairs when she heard scuffling and a man's angry, accented voice from the kitchen. "Where are they? Tell me or I'll hurt you more!"

Jo dashed back to her room. "Renata, lock this door. Don't open for anyone but me or JJ."

She rushed back down, silently making her way to the café door and peeked in the small window designed to avoid collision between multiple workers. She recognized the man as the F-250 guy. The bruises and makeshift bandages confirmed JJ had hurt him. He had Lily pressed against the wall. He held both her arms above her head with one hand and slapped her. It was obviously not the first time. "Where are they? Tell me or I'll hit you more."

"I don't know what you're talking about," Lily cried. "Stop hurting me."

Furious, Jo scanned the visible area for any item to use as a weapon. She spotted a cast iron skillet on the counter just inside the door. With a rapid two count, she burst through the door, grabbed the pan with both hands, and swung it as hard as possible into his head. The klong sound echoed and his hand released

Lily. He fell to the side with blood oozing through the bandana that was wrapped around his forehead. Lily's feet finally touched solid ground, but she was weak and crumpled to the floor. Jo rushed to Lily and knelt at her side, careful to support her head.

"Lily, it's me, Caroline," a familiar voice called out from the foyer. "Where are you?"

Jo turned toward the sound and hollered, "We're in the kitchen. We've got trouble." The noise next to Lily brought her attention back in time to see the F-250 guy scrambling to his feet and vanishing out the backdoor. "Caroline," Jo alerted. "He's gone out the back way."

Caroline gasped as she entered and rushed to Lily's other side. "Oh, my God. What happened? Here, let me help, Jo."

They leaned Lily back against the wall in a sitting position. Jo moved to the backdoor and set the deadbolt.

Lily's eyes fluttered as she muttered, "I didn't tell. I wouldn't tell him. I promised I wouldn't. I didn't…"

Caroline brushed her hands over her arms where bruises were already showing. "Lily, shush now. Try not to speak, honey. Let's get to the hospital and have them check you over."

Lily struggled to stand and shook off the aches, flexing her hands and arms as if taking inventory. "Like hell I am! I've got guests and they're owed breakfast. That's why this is called a bed and breakfast, Caroline."

Mary Lou, LouEllen, and Valerie arrived moments later and huddled at the doorway.

Mary Lou sarcastically commented, "A little early for sampling champagne, especially without us, isn't it, Lily? You couldn't hold off starting until we arrived for the meeting you scheduled."

Laughing, Jo filled in the ladies on the missing details and suggested they take Lily to a table in the dining room.

Lily stood with Jo's help and defiantly jutted out her chin. She picked up a towel and added cool water to dab at her face. "Okay, but I can walk."

Jo smiled. "I'd love to fix you breakfast, Brazilian style. You ladies, take a seat. I'll bring coffee. Then I'll run up and change before I start cooking." Jo raced upstairs. "Renata, open the door, it's me. I need my phone, and I want you by my side. I hope you like cooking."

"Is everything okay," Renata asked, "it sounded like something fell over."

"We're fine, but Lily was hurt a bit. I need to cook her breakfast and feed the rest of the podcasters. I'm going to set the dining sign to closed while they talk. Just stay with me."

"I will. I know a little cooking, so I can help."

They arrived back downstairs just in time to hear the exchange by Lily. "You're probably wondering why I called you here."

Inside the kitchen Jo placed a call. "JJ, they were here looking for the girls."

CHAPTER TWENTY-SIX

Saddle Up

JJ bristled as he reacted to the caller. "Wait! What? Attacked?" He listened, grinned, and cheered. "Good one. He hit you so turn around is fair play…Yes, I'll tell him, then we're on our way back…See you soon."

JJ disconnected and pocketed his phone. "Tommy, the Nacho guy that I flattened showed up at Flower looking for me. As a side act, he worked Lily over while demanding to find me. He got more intel than he planned. Jo clobbered him with a cast iron skillet, but the rat still slipped out the door. Gratifying that she whacked him though."

Tommy clucked his tongue. "I'll find the man and bring him in for questioning."

"Jo conked him, but he rebounded and took off when the podcast team showed up for breakfast. I'm sorry he's not laid out like a slab of meat for you to haul in. I recommend you swing by Flower and talk with Lily. You might display some concern toward these ladies. I'd expect their next podcast to be fiery if you don't coach 'em. You could pitch a few words and thoughts about the situation, so people don't get provoked into acting like vigilantes."

Annoyed, Tommy retorted, "If it isn't Madison giving me orders, it's some guest from Brazil telling me my business. I know my job. What are you supposed to do?"

JJ grinned and put up his hands. "Umm…I should provide that evidence you need? No more collateral damage? All good, right?"

Tommy's face nearly broke into a grin. He snapped, "No more problems until this mess is resolved, or I'm gonna box your ears. Both of you. Now get to work."

"Yes, sir."

"Tommy, dammit!"

JJ and Madison raced back to Flower and entered through the front door. JJ located Lily holding court with the podcasters in the dining room. He smiled as he approached the gaggle.

"Lily, Chief Tommy is coming to take your statement," JJ announced. "You might use this opportunity to give him a situation report with what's been happening. Ladies, please excuse me, I need to check on Jo after the ordeal. Madison, I'll catch up with you later."

Madison nodded and joined the women.

"Jo was sent upstairs along with the young'un," LouEllen stated. "They were going to try and make a Brazilian breakfast, but we intercepted. Anybody cooking anything in Lily's kitchen will only cause an anxiety attack. None of us wanted to deal with that fall-out."

JJ grinned and headed up the stairs. The door to their room was locked, so JJ quietly knocked and whispered, "Jo, it's me. Please open the door."

A flustered Jo poured through the door holding JJ tight.

"Honey, I've never done anything like that before. I was so mad at her being attacked I couldn't stop myself."

"Let's hope I never make you that mad. I'm not anxious to be clocked with an iron skillet. Come on, let's get Renata out the back before Chief Tommy shows up. I don't want to have to explain the girls to him until we have information to share."

Jo turned into the room. "Renata, honey, get your things. It's time to leave. We will take you to Hank's."

"Jo, I'm going to bring the rental to the back so we can load and go discreetly. If Nacho or his buddies are lurking around, pile into the car with Renata and lock it. I'll deal with him."

He pulled the car around. JJ looked everywhere. Nothing appeared amiss. He led Jo and Renata to the vehicle. They got in and crouched down while he loaded Renata's belongings.

"Jo, no one's following us. Call Hank and tell him our ETA."

When they pulled in, the couple was waiting outside.

JJ waved. "Hey, all. This is a wild morning."

"Renata and I wanted to see the horses. Camila, will you show us?" Jo asked in Spanish and left with them giving JJ's hand a quick squeeze."

JJ cleared his throat. "Can we go inside to talk? I've got news. It's not pleasant."

Once inside Hank demanded, "I know that tone. What's wrong?"

A grimly determined Hank listened as JJ outlined all the story pieces. Hank walked to a worn cupboard cabinet. From the highest shelf he popped a hidden door and pulled out a shoulder holster with a 1911 Colt .45 that he strapped on. He removed the weapon and released the clip to check the number of rounds. Satisfied the clip was full, he pushed it into the weapon and filled the holster.

"Never load a round in the chamber until you are ready to shoot," Hank growled. "Remember, friendly fire isn't. Don't put others at risk until the risk appears."

JJ nodded. "Safety first, especially with the girls around.

"I carry a .45 caliber derringer all the time," Ann added. "We're friendly folks, but that doesn't mean we trust everybody. This is one of those times when we saddle up for a fight. The girls are under our protection. No one takes them without a fight. Y'all call before driving up."

JJ swallowed and nodded. "Jo and I've got work to do to deliver the needed evidence to the chief. I know the girls are safe with you. Let's get Jo and the girls pried away from the horses. We'll say goodbye."

The three walked over and Camila showed off the horses she'd curried to JJ.

"You've done a great job with them. Show Renata how to help. Jo and I will be back as quick as we can."

The group retraced their steps to the house. Jo had an arm around each of the girls. JJ could see she tried to comfort them with caresses and laughter.

Jo embraced each girl and pleaded in Spanish. "Camila, Renata, we'll do everything we can to keep you out of Mateo's clutches. Stay here. Keep out of sight until we come back for you. Can you do that?"

Each girl teared a little but nodded agreement. Renata said, "Yes, Ms. Jo. Thank you and thank JJ, too."

JJ swooped Jo into an embrace after patting each of the girls on the shoulder and shaking Hank's hand. "Come on, Sherlock. We've work to do."

CHAPTER TWENTY-SEVEN

Fill in the Blanks

After Madison left, the podcast team chattered like a group of magpies. Lily, not in top form, struggled to get attention from the group. "Hey! I'm the one who got roughed up. Why is everyone willing to throw in the towel?" She noted each of the comments and protests with nods.

"We're not giving up," LouEllen argued. "Let's look at the evidence. Your charming guests helped bail out the podcast at each event this week. One got conked on the head. The other fought three assailants with weapons. You were cuffed around in your own kitchen. Does anyone else see a trend here?"

"We can't do our service if at any moment members of the goon squad are going to show up and hurt us," Caroline protested. "I didn't sign up to this civic cause to end up someone's punching bag."

Mary Lou shrugged in disgust. "Oh, do come along. Y'all are all packing, and you shoot like marksmen. You heard what Madison told us. If those jerks show up, they'll be arriving to a gun fight armed with a knife."

"Lily," Valerie cried, "I know you carry. Yet he got the drop on you."

"I got to admit, I wasn't situationally aware. I was busy preparing breakfast and suddenly he appeared. The back door didn't lock after I put out the trash."

"If they can come at you at any time of their choosing, what are we supposed to do?" Caroline questioned.

"Good morning, ladies."

They all turned to see Chief Tommy standing in the doorway. Several of them flinched, wondering what he'd heard. Tommy continued, "I see that your keen senses and intuition are in high gear, otherwise I'd have snuck up on you. I bet I surprised some of you."

Mary Lou, irritated and turning red in the face, scolded, "Oh good, someone from law enforcement sent a badge and gun to check on victims. Does this mean you're interested in a festering community problem?"

Not taking the bait, Tommy spoke to Lily. "I've a report that someone accosted you here. I'm told he wasn't a guest. Do you have any idea who he was or how he got in? You're methodical with keep doors locked."

"I don't know how he got in unless I forgot to engage the lock after taking out the trash. 'Course you told me before it's an easy lock to pick," Lily complained. "I was in the kitchen cutting produce. Suddenly, he grabbed me, shoved me against the wall, and slapped me. He demanded, "Where are they? Where are my girls?"

Tommy tilted his head, categorizing the information. "What girls?"

The podcasters sat silently, like clams hiding pearls, unwilling to share anything further.

Mary Lou broke first. "Go ahead, tell him, Lily. We're this far. Maybe with this puzzle piece, he'll finally help."

Lily watched Tommy's eyes trying to drill into her thoughts. "I told you to keep that secret until JJ gathered the final bit of evidence," Lily complained, her cheeks heating up from embarrassment. "Argh, I should know better than to confide in any of you."

Lily nearly laughed as Tommy's face looked like he'd swallowed a jar of beet juice mixed with lemon. His eyes never left her face.

Breaking, she confessed, "Jo and JJ found two teenagers who ran away from Mateo's human trafficking organization. JJ showed me how the kids were chipped and inventoried. Just a product to be bought and sold."

"Now isn't that ironic?" Valerie smirked. "Here's a couple on their vacation retreat just looking for some peace and quiet, yet they jump feet-first into our problems. JJ's out to get the proof points that Tommy here can't be bothered with because he thinks this is just a marketing game by us."

Tommy growled and shook his head. He clucked then bellowed, "Anything else going on with *Detective* JJ that I should know about? Is he planning to let me stay in office after he makes his arrests?"

LouEllen and Caroline looked down rather than face Chief Jager. LouEllen finally peered up with tears in her eyes. "We'll give you a favorable reference, Tommy."

Lily nodded agreement.

Tommy studied the silent ladies. "Grr. I'll work with JJ. You characters need to lock down your mouths for this next podcast. You know why. The enemies are listening. If you provide too much information, they'll try to escape, and proof-gathering will fail. They'll setup shop elsewhere. If they're trafficking humans, help me to support those kids." He waved his hands and added, "If they're safe for the moment, don't tell me where they are. I suspect that Jo will protect them like a mama cougar, which is better than child services while this gets sorted out."

All of them put on their game faces. Lily nodded. "Thanks, Tommy."

CHAPTER TWENTY-EIGHT

More Answers, New Questions

JJ answered the call and listened. "Sounds good, Madison. We'll meet you there." He disconnected. "Honey, Madison wants us to go with her to talk to Gloria to see if we can get an explanation for why the girls think she works for Mateo. Madison doesn't think it fits what she knows about Gloria since she arrived here. She will help Tommy with Gloria's workload, but she suggested that we stop at the hospital first to try and talk to her out of Tommy's hearing."

"I'll grab my bag, then we can go."

The two raced quietly down the stairs and out the door without getting noticed by the podcasters. Their meeting with Tommy seemed in full swing.

Once the rental car was rolling, Jo offered, "I can understand Madison's position since she's known Gloria for some time. I'm stuck on the look of terror on the girls' faces when they saw her. JJ, what're we missing?"

JJ glanced between Jo and the road. "If I didn't know better, one would think you're training as a first-rate analytic detective, my love. Does new focus mean when we get home you won't want to go back to the fame as the lead model for Destiny Fashions of Brazil?"

Jo blushed. "I still want to be a model. Can't a person pursue a second job as a detective, maybe parttime?"

JJ smirked thinking how popular she was to all the teens currently into fashion. Her fan mail was nearly equivalent to Santa Claus letter quantity during the Christmas season. "Jo, all detectives are armed in case the bad guys are looking for a fight. How are you going to always carry an eight-inch iron skillet around with those cute shorts and crop top?"

Jo laughed. "Maybe I get a holster like Hank to carry my weapon. My business card can read, *Have Skillet Will Travel*. He-he-he!"

They chuckled as JJ parked at the hospital and held Jo's hand as they walked from the parking lot. They bumped into Madison exiting the building.

"Gloria's gone," she grumbled. "She checked herself out of the hospital. I'm betting she's at the station. I'm heading that way. Care to come along, JJ?"

"I don't think so, Madison. Tommy's going to be there and, since the podcasters blabbed their secrets, Jo and I need to track down the last clues to make Tommy's case. Tell us how your discussion goes or call if we can help."

Madison nodded with a thoughtful expression.

"I know you don't believe she's not in this, Madison," JJ said. "If she's dirty, you'll be at risk confronting her. Be careful."

Madison shared a weak smile then turned and headed to her cruiser.

"Madison," Tommy complained, "at last, you're here. I can't believe how much nonsense flows into this place when Gloria's gone. Start with the phone calls and help me get the fires under control."

He caught the blank look on Madison's face. "No, I didn't get a call. She's not answering her phone. I just heard she checked herself out of the hospital. She can't be bothered checking into work like a responsible officer. You're deputized. Congratulations."

Before Tommy returned to his work, Madison cautioned, "Chief, we have a problem you need to know about. The podcaster ladies told you about the chipped teens and potential human trafficking. But there's more. The girls froze the night of the podcast when they saw Gloria. One of them vanished. The other stated Gloria works for Mateo."

Tommy cocked his head and looked at Madison, waiting for her to laugh. "What! She's in this mess? Is this why Gloria is missing? Mateo's thugs must have delivered a fake beating to maintain her cover. What's the proof?"

Tommy glared at Madison seeing doubt in her eyes, then demanded, "You don't believe it. I don't buy it. But I can't overlook the evidence that JJ is accumulating. Please set the phones to auto answer. I want answers. We start by locating Gloria. As soon as one of us gets her, haul her here. We'll check in every thirty minutes. You take your cruiser. I'll take mine."

Madison hesitated. "Tommy, I don't want this to be true about Gloria. I'm sure there's another answer. We just don't know it yet. I'm going to help JJ anyway I can."

"Don't get me wrong, Madison. I'm glad he is on our side. I don't know his professional background, as somehow, it's masked. All I know is, he works for a Brazil information protection services company. He's no fool. Someone trained him and he's got natural instincts. But I'll be glad when he's gone."

CHAPTER TWENTY-NINE

Five Second Fences

JJ parked his car at Flower and placed a quick call. "Hank, this is JJ. Do you know how many guard dogs are at the Mateo compound? Are there two, three, or hundreds?"

Hank snickered. "Maybe three. Not hundreds. Why?"

"I'm doing some recon work at that compound. I wasn't planning to ask permission or wrangle with nasty canines. I, uh… accidently dropped something there the evening we stopped to chat. I'd like to retrieve it with limited fuss."

"JJ, the last time I did repairs that bordered the compound, I counted three hundred-pound dogs—all with attitudes. Unless you're calling in extra resources to lay down suppressive fire to soften the area up, I'd consider your item lost."

JJ chuckled. "Great suggestions. I had something a little more subtle and not quite as noisy in mind. I presume that you might have access to Xylazine or Telazol or maybe Ketamine with your livestock. Is that correct??"

Hank was silent for a moment. "Yeah, I do. My vet gives me Ketamine prescriptions to use when I transport the horses. Most get nervous being led into the trailer. Why?"

"I'd like to use some if needed to enter the compound," JJ advised. "I plan to be in and out if the dogs are kept at bay. I can be there in half an hour if that gives you enough time."

Hank let loose a long sigh. "Alright. If your plan doesn't work, those hounds can reach the wall in six seconds. Plan to neutralize them in less than five."

JJ disconnected. Jo chuckled, then leaned in for a quick kiss. He got out and walked around to open her door. They held hands walking in the front door of Flower and headed toward the kitchen. JJ called out, "Lily, it's us. I've a favor to ask, if your meeting is finished."

Lily stopped chopping the veggies for the evening salad. "It's over. Tommy came in and gave us hell. He finally thinks we make be onto something, though his comments about you were a mixed bag of admiration and condemnation. Whatcha need, young man?"

JJ shrugged. "Do you have any extra substandard cuts of meat you can donate for a worthy cause?"

Lily snorted and grinned. "Poor cuts of meat? At my Flower? For my guests?" Lily scanned the area to verify no one was lurking or listening. Getting close to JJ, she whispered, "Between you and me, I bought a box from one of the truck sale outfits that knocked on the door offering a great deal." Wiggling her eyebrows, she asked, "How much can you take off my hands?"

JJ sniggered. "I'd like four of the thickest crummy steaks fired up and wrapped to go. Medium rare should work. The scent of the meat goes further when it's slightly cooked. We're headed to a potluck party and can't arrive empty handed."

Lily hesitated momentarily and looked up as if saying a prayer. She waved her hand in the air. "You're right. I don't want to know any details."

Jo and JJ, armed with their culinary treats, drove to Hank's making certain they weren't followed. Jo waved to the girls who were at an upstairs window. Hank greeted them at their car through JJ's lowered his window. "Almost thirty minutes on the nose. Here's the Ketamine, JJ. What do you have in mind?"

"Hank, can we turn this tranquilizer into a paste?" JJ unwrapped one of the foil packages of beef. "I want to frost these savory snacks for the four-legged guards who work so hard."

Hank guffawed for a few seconds. "I can add a bit of water for you, sure. Let's go up on the porch and use the table." Snickering again, he said, "You're calling on those pups with gifts they can't refuse."

Getting out to work with Hank while the girls rushed to Jo's window for a moment. JJ shrugged his shoulders. "Nobody seems to appreciate guard dogs. I'd like to help change that attitude."

Jo patted the girls and shooed them inside the house. JJ returned to the car with the doctored tidbits. He attached his seatbelt and started the car.

Jo rested her left hand on his right. "JJ, please say you have an alternative plan beyond the half-cooked steaks? What if they're trained not to take food from strangers?"

JJ smirked. "Then I've got to learn to clear that eight-foot fence in five seconds. Don't worry, honey."

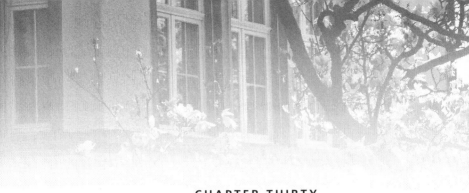

CHAPTER THIRTY

The Truth Please

Cleared of the compound, JJ placed a call. "Madison, where can we meet? I got the crittercams."

"I'm at the station. Tommy's still hunting for Gloria. Bring 'em here and let's look."

A short time later, JJ parked at the courthouse. He opened Jo's door. She exited like a cat stretching and gave him a quick squeeze. She passed him part of their treasure. JJ grabbed her hand, and they proceeded to the entrance.

"Hi, Madison," Jo excitedly said. "JJ got 'em, and the puppies are resting on full tummies. It was so exciting."

"Madison, can I show these on your computer, or should I set them up on mine?" JJ asked. "We have the recording since we set them up during Mateo's party to an hour ago. Hopefully all the data is there for that period."

"Over here. I can hook us to the big monitor so we can all see. We should have storage for five days of video."

JJ rigged the connections for the devices to Madison's machine. Each of the devices had an assigned quadrant for its display. The big screen blossomed into color, then greys and shadows when the playback began. At first, not many changes appeared. Then the units showed several people arriving in multiple vehicles and entering the residence.

"That must be the visitors," JJ commented. "Perhaps some of them are buyers."

Some of the cameras' video were blocked by hound dog noses for a short time and then were watered by three-footed salutes.

Staring at the images, Madison chuckled. "How did you get past the dogs, JJ, to get our cameras out? Jo suggested sleeping dogs when you arrived."

"Dogs are like people after a Christmas feast," JJ confessed. "Puppies love a good nap after a big meal of steak coated with Ketamine."

Madison stopped giggling and pointed at the top right frame. "There! That's Gloria's car. Look, she's getting out. Is this before the beating or after?" They frowned and groaned as they watched her petting the dogs like they were old friends.

Jo sniffled. "Not a very encouraging sight." She indicated the numbers running under the images. "Appears like it's timestamped shortly after these were installed, JJ."

JJ nodded. "Let's keep the film rolling… Hey, there's my friends. The three stooges from the bar fracas. Good to see one of them carries a limp. Too bad there's no sound on this video. I'd like to hear this conversation…likely complaints and comments about my demise."

"There's Gloria again," said Madison. "Hmmm. Looks like some anger exploding. With those bandages, she must have headed here after she left the hospital. No wonder we couldn't find her."

"The time/date stamp agrees with you, Madison," JJ confirmed.

"Wait for it…wait for it… There!" Madison cheered. "She's dressing Mateo down about something. Wish I could lip read. We can send it to an expert. Judging by her gestures and facial features, she's furious. Nothing ever works right when you piss off a lady with police training. Whoa! That's a bitch slap if ever

I've seen one." She murmured, "Sadly, I've seen plenty of them. Usually from the wrong side of things."

"Looks like Mateo is doing the shouting himself," Jo commented. "JJ, do you agree that is the stance of an angry man? I so agree with wanting sound."

JJ saw the frustration cross her face. Madison looked so sad. JJ mused, "It seems something's changed in their relationship. Mateo is decidedly calling the shots. Look at her face. She's mad but not willing to continue the argument. She's going to accept the rebuke and soldier on. What a shame."

"Without sound this whole thing is conjecture from our side," Madison protested. "Come on. We're going to find her and make her explain. I can hardly believe my eyes but I'm not willing to accept she's a bad cop. At least not yet."

JJ looked at Jo then turned toward Madison. "We want to believe your friend's not in on this trafficking operation. However, the evidence suggests otherwise."

Madison growled, "At least let us confront her before we go to Tommy. Guilty or not, I want to hear the truth from her own mouth."

"I'd prefer to hear she's not guilty," admitted Jo. "I warmed to her when we met, but the terror from Camila and Renata…"

"Then we're in violent agreement," JJ stated. "We want the truth."

"At least I know where to find her," Madison added.

Gloria sat, listlessly staring off into space at her favorite table in Really Good. Her mind traced her missteps, anger, and doubt. She had no way out of this mess without risking those she loved. Keeping her secret was the only way she thought would work in the long run. She knew the game wardens, rangers, police, and even border patrol, recommended this place and at one time felt like she fit. She appreciated the coffee at Lily's Flower, but she felt included here. Harry sometimes offered specials to law enforcement folks. The tables were small, but the only booth at the back Harry used for special folks, was empty. Gloria hadn't seen them enter and her face reflected surprise as the trio slid into chairs. They blocked her exit—hemming her in. Madison's jaw muscles were clenching and unclenching, highlighting her agitated state. Gloria sucked in a breath and then looked in the dark pool of coffee in her cup.

"My friend, I think it's time to come clean and tell us everything. Let's start with why you're working for Mateo."

Gloria fiddled with her cup. She muttered, "I don't know what you're talking about." Then she glanced at the dark eyes of JJ with his grim expression and sneered, "You again. Did you put her up to this? What fabricated lies are you peddling?"

JJ methodically opened his laptop. Without saying a word, he launched the first video. Gloria took a breath and felt her heart lurch. Her breathing turned irregular and ragged viewing the video and listening to JJ narration.

JJ provided commentary. "Here at Mateo's, just after you checked yourself out of the hospital, we find you petting the guard dogs like best buddies. Next, you're pissed about something and getting into his face. Then he hauls off and bitch-slaps you to the ground. We're hoping you'll fill in the blanks about your employer-employee discussion before we take it to the chief."

Gloria brought her hands to her face and wept. She felt her mind race as she searched for answers. Sensing her defeat her sobs escalated before finally facing her accusers. She realized there was no way out.

"Two escaped girls claim you're the one who handles the trafficking details for Mateo," Jo mentioned.

Gloria moaned and nodded; tears streaked her face as the words reigning down felt worse than a beating.

"How could you, Gloria?" Madison, her face turning red to purple, demanded, "I know your parents. They immigrated here from Mexico. Gaining their citizenship was a huge milestone. You're first generation American. Why would you do this dishonor to your parents?"

Gloria sat up and angrily wiped the tears. She blew her nose with a paper napkin. "You don't know anything. What would you do to save the lives of your parents? What if your ranch sits at the Texas/Mexican border with only the Rio Grande separating the countries? Mateo has a huge hacienda in Mexico where he stages his operation there to bring his slave inventory here to sell. He brings young boys and girls who are forced to do unthinkable things for money." Gloria took a breath and blew her nose again, anger capturing her emotions. "It sickened me when he captured my parents and took over our ranch. Yeah, he did it right after I finished my training and was hired on in Magnolia Bluff. Each time I've tried to confront the man or demand to see my parents, he showed pictures of those he's killed and buried on our ranch, ready to frame me if I stepped out of line."

"Your parents are captives on their own ranch?" Madison echoed. "He's blackmailing you?"

"I was proud to take my badge home to show Papa." Gloria groaned. "My badge is on the line. If I'm labeled a dirty cop, I won't get to do the job I love. Then there's jail time that he'll help orchestrate."

JJ softened his tone as he asked, "And the three stooges? Was their escape part of the exercise? You kept me talking so they could get positioned to jump me, right?"

Gloria drew in another ragged breath and shook her head. "I'm so sorry. I was told to delay you from leaving. I had no idea what Mateo planned. Their escape was my fault. I figured they would play along and go peaceably into a cell until you left. I was wrong. You'll be happy to know every hit hurt."

Gloria looked at the cup that Jo must have replaced with fresh. She took a sip. "Thank you, Jo. I never touched the girls and kept them off the auction block. Those teens would have no way of knowing this, but I didn't want them as hookers...or worse. I hoped I could save these two; I knew I couldn't save them all." She looked between JJ and Madison. "What happens now?"

"I promised Chief Jager my evidence, which includes you," JJ said. "None of us wanted to believe you were involved."

"I understand you were put in a horrible position," Madison added. "I wish you'd have come to me or even Tommy. We're going to need his help."

JJ nodded. "I think we'll get it after all of this information is on his desk."

"Are the girls alright?" Gloria asked. "Mateo's furious about losing them because of the size of the deposit he received."

Jo patted the top of Gloria's hand. "They're hidden and safe."

"Let's get you to the station," JJ advised. "The last podcast is starting soon. If Mateo's that angry, I think tech support is gonna be in high demand. We'll head over once the show is finished. Madison, tell Tommy I'll bring the last of the details he'll need for arrests."

"Madison, do you need my help taking Gloria to the station?" Jo asked.

"I'm not handcuffing her, if that's what you're asking. Gloria, give me your word you'll not run."

Gloria, bordering on tears, replied, "I am done hiding. Let's go."

CHAPTER THIRTY-ONE

Of Rats and Cheaters

JJ pulled up to the Head Case Salon with minutes to spare before the scheduled start time. Jo grabbed his laptop as he opened her door. The crowd on the sidewalk milled around with a sense of excitement.

"Excuse me, sir, ma'am," JJ and Jo offered multiple times as they work their way through the throng of watchers.

Head Case owner, Daphne Leigh, was dressed in a lovely, fitted dress of purple, with matching tendrils framing her face. Her makeup and lipstick made her appear almost sophisticated until she frantically waved at them to hurry. "Folks, come on, let them through, please. We need their help to get this show moving." She tucked JJ's free hand into her elbow and dragged him into her shop. The front room contained flowers, brochures, and photos of Magnolia Bluff women who utilized her services. A couple of leather couches offered a comfortable waiting area. JJ noted, the podcast team was set up and ready.

"JJ, this is the biggest crowd yet," Jo said. "They are so tightly packed against the window. It's wild. Hey look, that lady is waving at you, honey."

JJ grinned at Jo, shaking his head.

The ladies hosting this live stream look relieved as they spotted him. Mary Lou gave JJ a sly smile and a deferring nod.

One of the patrons waiting for her perm time to end called to Daphne and motioned to her for help. She whispered, "Daphne, that the computer genius? He's so handsome—just dreamy. If I was twenty years younger..."

Daphne chuckled. She tactfully leaned closer to her patron who sported an extra forty pounds and grey roots. "Susan, see that slim, dark-haired beauty next to him? She's your competition. All natural, too. I'm told she wields a mean cast iron skillet when she feels wronged. Be careful where you tread, my friend." The woman nodded and returned to her gossip-filled magazine.

"Father Gorman," Mary Lou announced, "we're live in five, four, three, two, and...one."

The preacher started, "Welcome to Magnolia Bluff..."

The door opened and a thrown object clunked as it hit the floor and rolled several feet. Thick smoke spewed from it. Patrons panicked by the smoke.

An unknown voice incited the pandemonium, "Fire! Fire!"

The building disgorged the people, equipment, personal belongings left behind. A different voice shouted, "Someone get the fire department!"

JJ shoved Jo toward the opening noting the minimal pushing, but fast feet. He turned to verify Mary Lou could manage her wheelchair. She'd gotten entangled on the cords running the equipment.

"Jo, go on. Try to keep folks away from the entrance maybe onto the street. I'm gonna help Mary Lou. People gave the entrance a wide berth but remained close enough to see what happened.

JJ wheeled Mary Lou safely outside into the circle of her team. He punched 911, listened, and hit it again. "I can't get through. I guess everyone is calling." He peered up at the noise from a siren. "Wow, that's unbelievable to have a fire truck here already. This must be the world's best emergency service ever constructed."

"JJ, this is a volunteer fire department," Jo noted. "It would be beyond amazing if they could respond so fast. It's too neat."

JJ looked across the sea of people and saw his three assailants lounging against the familiar F-250 truck parked out of the way. JJ moved toward them with a determined stride. Jo tugged at his arm. "JJ, don't go there. Some innocent bystanders might get hurt."

He shook off her hand. Before he got close enough, they discreetly displayed their pistols, so JJ held his ground. Frustrated, he watched them load up and leave with satisfied looks and hand gestures.

The firefighters rushed into the salon searching for the fire. Moments later, the tallest man, with Fire Chief on his hat, walked out. "It's a smoke grenade, that's all. Open the doors, Daphne, and turn on a couple of the fans. The air will clear in short order, and you can resume business."

JJ approached the chief. "When did you receive the call? Your team arrived right after it started."

The fire chief took off his hat and ruffled his brown hair while he looked JJ over. "It arrived twelve minutes ago. Something about the caller seemed off. I usually get callers who are over-excited or rattled to the point where their speech makes no sense. I wasn't sure what to expect when the person claimed fire was spreading everywhere and to enter the salon with the hoses going. No one tells this team how to put out a fire."

Daphne danced around at the news, kissing a couple of the firemen as they exited. "Woo-hoo! I still get my ad space on the podcast. My Saturday business isn't going to be ruined. I liked that second kisser. I wonder if he's married."

JJ looked around and mentally listed the inconsistencies of this event compared to the others. He thought, *This failed to stop the show, but why?* He and Jo reentered the salon, opened the back windows toward the rear exit, and started fans to dissipate the smoke.

The hosts of the show filed inside and looked toward their equipment.

JJ walked back from the storage area at the rear of the salon. "Ladies, the air is clear, and no one is coughing. Good news. Are you podcast mavens ready to resume?"

The ladies straightened up, threw their shoulders back, and strutted to their seats, reminding JJ of roosters about to announce the sunrise. Mics were checked and the program launched with Father Gorman completing the introduction.

"Folks, sorry the podcast was late, the disrupters plagued us again," Mary Lou started. "Valerie, the more attacks we get the more information we need to ferret out."

"You are so right, Mary Lou. We can't prove the identity of the attackers, but we know it's Mateo and his thugs."

The two ladies bantered back and forth, heaping venom on their foes, while stopping short of swearing on open mic.

"Mary Lou," Caroline commented, "as spineless as these people are, our community needs to feel safe. We started this series of podcasts trying to learn more about our newest neighbors. We invited Mateo Hernandez to explain his goals in the community, but he refused. He might even try to sue us, but then we'd get the information at court. What do you think, LouEllen?"

"Private property or not, something stinks with the set-up. I don't know for certain, but this is ranch and farm country that don't need walls to hide behind. Let's field questions and comments from our listeners."

Callers cited the same concerns. Mary Lou made a plea for letters to their state representatives to consider a bigger investigation.

Cheers and applause ended the show after Daphne announced a free shampoo and blow dry with every hair cut during the next thirty days.

Jo assisted JJ with his equipment. "Honey, do you find it odd there was no cyberattack this time? It makes me curious."

"I'm waiting for the other shoe to fall," JJ mused. "The fire chief said the call came at least ten minutes lead time before the grenade was launched. The caller begged for hoses to be spraying when they entered because of the rapidly spreading fire. I think Mateo's hit men expected everything to be ruined with water so why bother with a technology hit?"

Jo snickered. "Best laid plans of rats and cheaters often go awry."

JJ hugged her and laughed along with her.

CHAPTER THIRTY-TWO

Down to Brass Tacks

JJ looked lovingly at Jo. "I think we've got enough evidence for Tommy. Let's deliver it, answer any questions, and bow out. I'm thinking hot tub time at Flower with bubbly and no interruptions."

"I'm glad Tommy will handle this mess, but I think we've other loose ends that may delay our romantic bath."

"What? I thought you'd be delighted."

"I want to spend time with you, so don't look so sad. We need to follow up on Gloria's claim. Her story broke my heart. I am concerned about Camila and Renata. I can't rest until I know they'll be taken care of. We can't stop now."

"You're right. I just want our vacation time back. None of this was part of my plan. I'll extend our time and alert folks back home."

"Let's take everything except the location of the girls to Tommy and then decide the next step."

"Sometimes, my dear, you are so smart. You're really getting into this detective thing." He leaned over and kissed her cheek. "I'm holding you for the more-of-us time later."

Jo playfully kissed him back. "Let's do this, sweetheart."

The parking lot was nearly deserted as the evening shadows took the places of vehicles. JJ parked the rental and opened the door, giving Jo a hand. "They roll the sidewalks up early during the week in small towns, Jo."

"The small town is showing. I hear insect night chatter that I've never heard before. I like new stuff." She handed JJ his laptop containing the valuable information and took his hand to walk to the door to the station.

"Uh-oh," whispered JJ, spotting Madison standing at attention inside the small, windowed conference room at the far end.

Tommy raised his finger like he was disciplining kids. His face was beet red. "How could either of you think for a second not to tell me…" The angry words intermittently penetrating the closed room aligned to his volume.

"JJ, should we leave for now?" Jo cringed at the next outburst.

"Gloria, I believed this job meant something to you. We talked about trust when I interviewed you. You said…" Tommy raked his hair as he marched back and forth.

"I think we can wait. He's slowing his pacing. Gloria and Madison haven't broken yet. That's a good sign," JJ whispered.

Jo punched his shoulder. "You brute. You're just glad Tommy's not focused on you."

"Ya got that right. Watch it, he's turning and—"

Tommy froze, catching sight of the audience. He shifted, commented too quietly for JJ to hear. The deputies turned and spotted the diversion.

"JJ, let's come back tomorrow."

Agitated, Tommy pointed two fingers at them, then motioned toward the empty chairs inside.

"Jo, I think we've been summoned to join the party. We'll deliver our information then duck out."

They entered and sat as indicated, with the deputies joining them at the table.

"As a recap for our guest detectives," Tommy grumbled, "we've experienced a failure to communicate. That ends now. I'm the chief. I want all the information. Everything you think or know is going on—shady or not. I decide the next steps and additional investigation avenues. No more secrets, folks."

"We understand, sir. Jo and I brought you—"

"Give me a sec." Tommy took a couple of deep cleansing breaths and refocused. "JJ, show me what you have. Then I'll make one of two calls. As folks say today, I want it transparent, son."

JJ connected his laptop to the wall screen in the room. "This is the list of the cyberattacks including the threatening messages to the members of the podcast group and the owners of the venues. The crittercam videos show the compound visitors, including Gloria, and the results of her argument with Mateo. These are the pictures of the chipped girls. The inventory sheets of the teens tracked through this place is incomplete." JJ took a breath, reached for a bottle of water in the center of the table, and took a drink. "I've written up the event outside of the compound with the man I called Nacho, and the additional encounters including the fight behind the bar that Gloria can confirm. Jo wrote up Nacho's intrusion at Flower, his manhandling of Lily, and Jo clocking him. Neither Jo nor I have real details from when she was knocked down in the alley, but I've included a photo of the threat note left behind. The original is back at Flower if needed."

"Where are the girls?" Tommy demanded.

"I'd rather not tell you for now, Chief. Mateo's still hunting them, as Gloria probably told you. They're safe for the time being."

"I'll bring them to you when that Mateo creature is in custody," Jo commented.

Tommy shook his head. JJ noticed the angry lines forming on his face and his lips thinning into a tight line. JJ felt he might lash out in anger.

Tommy grabbed the conference phone and punched in a number, eyeing the four while waiting. "Sam, it's been a while. Do we have time for pleasantries or should I get to the point?... I figured. We're still alike. Here's the deal. My newest deputy's been undercover trying to get details for a possible human trafficking marketplace here in Magnolia Bluff. We think the staging on this side of the border is close to Nueva Laredo. We think a local ranch was commandeered with the owners held as hostages. How much pecan whiskey do I need to send you to investigate?" Tommy's face paled. He dropped into the last available chair. "That much, huh? Do I need to add some of our bar-b-que to go with that bribe? We've got the best in Texas... No need to get your jeans in a bunch. I'm teasing you about the b word. I know the illegal immigration problems along the border have taken your sense of humor." He listened, then nodded. "I'm in kind of a hurry. I'll text you the ranch address and GPS coordinates. Tell your people to take care. These varmints have already worked over my deputy. I don't want more people hurt. Appreciate you, bro. Talk soon."

Tommy fingered a text and handed his cell to Gloria to verify before hitting send.

"If this report comes back as bogus, Gloria goes to jail. If it's true and her parents are safe, we charge the compound and take care of the scum by the book."

Tommy stood giving everyone permission to follow suit. "JJ, you did a good job assembling the information. Thank you."

CHAPTER THIRTY-THREE

Who's My Backup?

"**C**hief, I expected you to shout at us for meddling in your town affairs, but Jo and I are pleased to provide you the needed information. Madison's great support helped immensely with the girls. We hope Gloria's issues get resolved with what your contact finds. I'm certain it will come together for the truth you want."

"Agreed. I'm calling for backup support. I'd like you to stick around for when we storm the compound. I don't want to take any chances."

Tommy refocused on the call. "Hello, dispatch, this is Chief Tommy Jager in Magnolia Bluff. I'm hoping you can loan me some Rangers for an operation tomorrow on a suspected human trafficking location. How many resources can you have here by dawn?" He rolled his eyes to the team.

JJ wondered if the chief could get support on such short notice. *Mateo didn't strike him as a patient man. Tommy was looking a bit exasperated, too.*

"Young lady, please connect me with Romeo Stanton," Tommy insisted. "I'll explain what I need to him…I appreciate that Saturday night is for fun, but ya know criminals don't take time off. I'd like two Rangers here in the morning, early."

Tommy shook his head in disgust. "Thanks. I'll take Tuesday or Wednesday at the latest, ma'am. This is not a kiddie party and I need seasoned personnel…Fine. This number is good to call day or night. Even Saturday night…No, ma'am. Goodnight." He ended the call with a slap of his hand on the table. "I'll tell you what, she'd score zero on that survey. Dang it."

"Tommy, I'll call Dad and ask his help," Madison offered. "Even a retired Texas Ranger would love a chance to work again."

"Madison, I want to hit that place in the morning. I don't want them sneaking out and escaping. Thanks. Do it."

Madison pulled out her phone and dialed. "Hi, Dad. Are you game for a little action?" She leaned back in her chair as if waiting for a long reply then groaned. "No, Dad, not that kind of action. I'm glad you aren't on speaker phone. I'm talking about the investigative kind that calls for Ranger expertise against possible human traffickers…" Shaking her head, she grumbled. "Men…Yes, Dad, you. Magnolia Bluff needs your help in the morning. Possible firefight. I suggested to Chief Jager you might help as your old headquarters are too busy—"

Tommy hollered, "Hey, Grant, bring any Ranger friends you know."

Madison nodded. "Did you hear Tommy, Dad?…Good. Thank you. See you at dawn at the station in Magnolia Bluff…Yes, Dad. I'll bring extra coffee and snag some donuts from Flower. Good night."

"JJ. Jo," Tommy started with a serious tone and a facial expression to match. "Being civilians, you can't be part of the team that enters the complex. I'd like you outside on the perimeter in case we get a runner."

They grinned, and JJ added, "We're in. Thanks for including us."

"After we round up the guys at that place, you need to surrender the girls. I'll turn them over to CPS or HLS, although Homeland Security is not my first choice."

Jo's face fell. "What's CPS?"

"Child Protective Services. They protect kids and families. I trust them and know one of the local case workers."

Jo cast an uneasy look at JJ.

CHAPTER THIRTY-FOUR

Everyone Goes Home

JJ parked in front and watched for someone to arrive to unlock the doors. The soft blue and pink glow of dawn complemented the mood for potentially saving children. Gloria drove up and danced a two-step singing her favorite country tune as she waved. She unlocked the door and turned on the lights. JJ and Jo entered minutes later armed with coffee and pastries.

"I'm glad you two brought some food. I was in such a hurry this morning I didn't eat. Sleep last night was easier, thinking my parents might be safe today."

JJ liked that Gloria seemed a little lighter on her responses—more confident. "Gloria, when this business is finished, maybe you can work on more important cases than donut thieves."

Jo grinned. "Did you catch the sweet crook?"

"Nope. We don't have many security cameras, and the culprit was cagey."

A distinctive engine sound indicated more arrivals. "I bet that's the chief; he needs a tune-up on his cruiser something fierce."

Tommy sauntered in followed by Madison and Grant.

"Hi, Mr. Jackson. Are any of your friends coming along?"

"No, I don't think so. Sorry, Tommy. I did put the word out so we might get surprised. But you know the old saying, one riot, one Ranger."

JJ noticed the incredulous look on Tommy's face.

"Yeah I know, but it's always a fun line to offer in a tight situation," Grant added.

Tommy shrugged which JJ took as resolve. "Grant, this is JJ and Jo. They're civilians visiting Magnolia Bluff who helped get us to this point. The best part is they brought the goodies."

JJ and Jo shook hands with the former Ranger. "Nice to meet you, sir," JJ offered.

Tommy set his hat on the table then grabbed a coffee and a couple of sweet rolls. "Thank you for bringing snacks. I'll pay you back later."

Everyone settled around the table.

Tommy cleared his throat. "Thanks for coming. Let's talk about how I see this going down. We drive in quiet and park by the clump of trees on the gate side. We don't want to panic them or make them believe we have an army. I learned from Gus that the cameras Mateo ordered are still on backorder. He might have a guard maybe at the gate and there's still the dogs to consider."

"The dogs are big," JJ mentioned.

"Good to know. JJ, I want you and Jo to walk down the fence line on the left side as that is closest to the buildings. If there are chip implants, like in the girls, you might be able to pick 'em up. If you locate any, text Madison. I plan to do the main talking with Gloria by my side to fake him out. I'll say we're there to do an inspection as a follow-up on the citizen complaints of gun fire to close the case Madison opened. Gloria, you can do a smile and wink thing like you have it under control, so he doesn't suspect anything."

She nodded.

"I have a warrant from our judge, but I'd like to avoid using it if they are willing to show us around."

"I know from the last podcast and our experience when we got lost, that these creeps are armed. I suggest caution," advised JJ.

Tommy nodded agreement and looked at everyone. "I'll be on point. Let's not bunch together, and keep your eyes moving, especially in case their guard dogs are lurking on patrol."

"Mateo will believe I'm in his control, if I'm positioned on the side." Gloria smirked. "Plus, I've got weighted nets we can use for the dogs, but they also respond to commands, and I know them."

Madison breathed a sigh of relief, louder than planned, and everyone looked at her with grins.

Grant straightened up and smoothed his crown of white hair with his huge hands. "Tommy, I like your plan. Sounds like one my team made for a similar situation. You can't plan for this greedy creep to greet you with open arms. If he's guilty, he won't let you rummage around and trip over something he's hiding." Grant's leadership was evident to the folks around the table as he continued, "Here's someone with an organization dedicated to acquiring and processing people for sale to the highest bidder. He surrounds himself with armed guards ready to enforce his bidding. I expect him to lure us inside for an ambush if we get near the front door. Furthermore, I'm surprised that you want to include the civilians where bullets could fly. They're bright folks but this invasion is risky…"

Music from JJ's cell phone halted the discussion. He showed Jo the incoming tag, and she paled as he answered the call. "Hank, what's up? Is everything okay?" JJ shifted the call to the device's speaker.

Ann, Hank's wife, cried, "JJ, three men knocked on the door a short time ago demanding the girls. Hank barked at them in Spanish and ordered them off the property. They shot him.

We're holed up in the house, staying away from the windows. We need help. Can you reach out—"

"Ann, it's Chief Jager in Magnolia Bluff. Keep that security bar engaged 'til we arrive. I've assembled a team that can help. Are they still outdoors?"

"I hear shots now and again at the house. It's likely they want us pinned down, but I'm not sure."

"Tell that ornery husband of yours to stay alive until we get there. I've got Madison and Grant with me, too. Gloria already called for an ambulance."

Everyone stood. Gloria pulled open a drawer and passed around bullet-proof tactical vests. Tommy rushed over to unlock the weapons cabinet and handed out weapons. He started to hand a weapon to JJ. "Son, how are you with a semi-automatic rifle?"

"I've never trained with one. I'm great with pistols if you have one."

Tommy appeared astonished. "Really, I found something you can't do? Take my service revolver but stay back. Don't shoot me by mistake.

"Let's get going. Drive with lights and sirens like the helicopters did in that Vietnam movie. Fan out fast and we'll ask them to surrender. Take no chances before they're handcuffed or dead."

"Tommy, JJ and I will work our way around to the back of the house and help secure the girls."

Grant smirked. "JJ, that's one bold lady you've got. My Madison's the same. I always liked strong females."

Madison blushed with pride.

"JJ, why didn't you tell me the girls were there?" complained Tommy.

CHAPTER THIRTY-FIVE

The Eyes in the Sky

M adison, with Grant in the passenger seat, tailgated the chief, and JJ bringing up the rear. Sirens provided distraction. As they turned into Hank's ranch road, the dust acted like a cloak while they exited their vehicles and spread out using available cover. JJ and Jo remained behind the vehicles as instructed.

Grant grabbed the bull horn and, sounding like God from above, shouted, "Texas Rangers. Weapons down. Hands in the air. The coroner's on his way. Your choice."

Two shots were fired in response from behind the equipment storage building located away from the house. With the dust thick in the air, the projectiles sailed over their heads. Tommy motioned for everyone to spread out as he approached toward the direction of the muzzle flash.

Jo stayed low behind the vehicle. JJ picked his way from stone to bush, toward the back of the house until he vanished around the corner.

Two white vehicles with flashing lights of red and blue pulled through the gate parking perpendicular to the buildings. Two men exited using the car as a shield. One man called out, "Thought we heard shots. We're looking for Chief Jager. Is he here?"

"I'm here. Turn off the lights. The dust you raised won't last long. Who are you?"

"We're the Texas Rangers you requested, Stewart Hayes and Gordon Little." They ducked low, making their way toward the voice.

"Hayes and Little. Welcome. I'm Gloria, Tommy's deputy. It's Grant Jackson to your right. Tommy's up ahead. The owners are inside with the door barricaded. According to Hank's wife Ann, he's nursing a wound. I've been in that log cabin. Bullets won't penetrate those walls."

"Welcome, Rangers!" Tommy shouted. "Work your way to me if you can."

"Glad we're not too late to the party. Gordon and I are always up for a firefight on a Sunday morning."

The two cruisers moved forward, lights off, but a speaker boomed, "Tommy, it's Romeo. We're coming in!"

Bullets were fired from all sides. Five minutes later, it was silent. One assailant was facedown in the dirt, waiting for the coroner. Nacho and his associate were cuffed.

Tommy walked up to Romeo and shook his hand. "Your office said it was too busy to help, but I figured you'd listen to the message. I just didn't know when you'd arrive."

Romeo laughed. "You made it sound like work. Next time use the words 'dangerous but spirited entertainment', and we'll arm wrestle to get selected to attend."

"Point taken. This isn't the compound. We came here because the rancher's wife Ann called for help when her husband was shot. They're protecting two witnesses from the compound. The three we grabbed work for the compound owner, Mateo Hernandez. We need to go there. I already have a warrant."

"A two-fer. Alright. I'm leaving Libby here. She's my medic and can tend to any wounds and arrange for transport. Gentlemen and ladies, let's go clean up the trash at the other location."

JJ walked up. "Tommy, Jo has the girls inside. She and Ann are calming them down. I'm ready to go to the compound. We think they're holding others, but we don't know how many or where. The girls are too hysterical to talk." JJ approached Nacho. "How'd you find them? Only a few people knew the girls were here."

Nacho spat on JJ's shoes. "High resolution drones with eyes. You're not the only one who uses technology."

JJ backhanded him hard enough to sound like a firecracker. He turned and walked toward the remaining vehicle.

"JJ, we're going to put these two in Gloria's patrol car. I want you to stand guard. I've got enough Ranger muscle to clear the compound. Once we secure it, I'll ask you to come grade the situation."

"You don't want me to bring the girls to confirm the staging area, I hope."

"Nope. They don't need to ever see anything like this again."

JJ waited outside Hank's ranch listening for sounds of more shots. His phone chirped with a text from Jo asking to come out to talk to him. He responded *yes*.

Jo gave JJ a hug and held him a bit tighter than necessary. "I'm glad you're okay. I was worried. I've got the girls calmed down. Libby came in to work on Hank and gave Ann half a Valium for her nerves. She's rattled and upset about the girls."

"Gloria called for an ambulance before we left. It's en route. The coroner is about ten minutes out. I'm tasked with watching over these two while the compound is getting stormed."

"Two? I thought there were three."

JJ pointed to the lifeless figure by the car. Jo froze, staring at the bullet riddled body. JJ put his arm around her and whispered, "Do you hear that?"

Jo snapped her attention from the bloody sight. "Hear what?"

"It's been over twenty minutes since Tommy and the Rangers left. I've not heard a single shot. Something's wrong." JJ's phone chimed and he answered. "Chief, what's going on? I don't hear any shooting."

"JJ, have Gloria bring the car, you, and our two prisoners to Mateo's ranch house. Make Jo stay with the girls."

"That bad, huh?...Yes, she'll watch the girls and have the ambulance medics check everyone out. Libby is with Hank."

JJ kissed Jo's forehead then looked at the skyline. "Gloria," he called. "We need to get over to the compound."

CHAPTER THIRTY-SIX

Not Soon Enough, Not Too Late

Gloria parked near the front door of the compound's main house. In the light, JJ noticed the stonework on the outside looked expensive. The wrap-around porch made the two-story home look massive. The windows on the front had wrought iron bar work. This was a house built to command respect.

They exited and Gloria leaned against the car. The occupants weren't worth listening to. JJ took the steps to the open door. He heard voices as he entered.

"Tommy, it's JJ. Gloria's watching the prisoners."

Tommy walked from around the corner. He took his handkerchief out of his pocket and smeared some of the dirt off his sweaty face. "This place is disgusting. There are plates stacked everywhere in the kitchen. Empty glasses in the main rooms used for entertaining. It's filthy and no one in sight, so far." Tommy took a sip from his water bottle. "Son, I need you to sweep the area with your electronics for anything we missed." He ground his teeth and spit on the dirt. "Empty. No one left to accuse. No real proof."

The Rangers appeared like a crescent circle around Tommy.

JJ was struck at how similar the rangers looked: tall, imposing, and tough. He started walking around the room to his right. It contained fewer dirty dishes like Tommy mentioned, so perhaps not a place for guests.

"Romeo," Tommy muttered, "I'm sorry you didn't get the spirited fun we were expecting. I waited too long. It's my fault that—"

"Wait!" JJ hollered. "Tommy, something's registering under this rug."

Two men rushed over and rolled up the rug, exposing a trap door. They pulled it open to reveal inky darkness and an unbelievable stench.

"Weapons," whispered Romeo, causing a uniform unholstering of firearms.

Mewing sounds and groans filtered from the darkness. JJ rushed down the steps into the unknown. Moments later, his voice echoed, "Oh, my God! Nooo."

The men followed with flashlights, bringing horrors no one could imagine to light.

"No one should treat another human like this," Grant moaned.

JJ covered his mouth and nose with his handkerchief while he surveyed the victims, two or more per cot with no food or water visible. A bucket over-the-rim-full in the corner appeared to be the toilet. The stench was overpowering, bringing tears to his eyes and making his stomach roil.

Madison moved to check three children huddled on a cot in the back. Rail thin and dirty. They hadn't seen a shower in days, but they were alive.

"I've a pulse here on this young man," voiced JJ. "I need water."

A Ranger closest to the stairs, raced for water, pausing to empty the contents of his stomach and grabbing the bottle of Vicks from his fanny pack to spread under his nose.

"Here's some water, son," he said as he handed the bottle and a blue jar to JJ. "Swab a blob of this under your nose. It'll help."

JJ obeyed, fighting back his tears. "This is what it must have felt like for the Allied armies when they liberated death camps like Auschwitz."

JJ watched as Madison's fury threatened to shut her down. JJ had stepped over to help when Grant wrapped an arm around her. "Come on, honey, these kids need our help at this moment, not our anger. Put some Vicks on and pass it along."

"These kids over here are burning up with fever and can't stand," Hayes announced. "That may be why they were locked down here. Left to die. They need water and medical attention."

"Radio it to the team at Hank's," said Tommy.

JJ stepped over to check their hands for the scar and read the embedded chip. "Tommy, I've checked a bunch of these captives so far. They're all chipped. Some have been here for a week, others up to a month. I don't know what they are sick with, but this might the quarantine area.

"I'm on it," Tommy said, wiping his tears.

The last ambulance loaded up, the EMT stated, "Nice work. They're in bad shape, both sick and undernourished. They're being intubated for dehydration on-scene. We'll quarantine them to make sure these fevers aren't new virus imports we don't need on our soil."

"Thank you. I'll check with the doctors at County Hospital later in the day." Tommy looked at the worn-out team. "I need everyone back at my office to get the report pulled together while it is fresh on our minds. Hopefully, my buddy in Laredo with confirm the last piece of this puzzle."

JJ relayed his phone conversation with Jo. "Jo says she's not bringing the girls to you. She'll stay with them at Hank's until Ann returns. Tommy, she can't hand them over to strangers after all this. She believes they are traumatized after the last forty-eight-hours. I tend to agree with her."

A wave of anger surged through Tommy but then subsided like an ocean wave being pulled back into the sea. "You tell Jo I need her to bring the girls for their statements. I called Ann at the hospital. Hank's being released. They'll both be at my office. We'll talk through the options for the girls, with no snap decisions. And that's Chief Jager for now."

JJ texted Jo.

> Madison and I are coming to get you and the girls.
> Grant is riding in with his buddies. It'll be alright.
> Madison will help us.

CHAPTER THIRTY-SEVEN

Going Home

The mood in the station was like a heavy shroud drenched in disbelief. Tommy motioned folks into the conference room, and they settled into chairs. Jo and Madison arrived last with the girls. Hank, with his arm in a sling, commented, "Ann, let's sit next to the girls." He shifted his chair and patted each girl on the shoulder. Ann got up and hugged them.

Gloria appeared at the doorway. "Chief, the prisoners are secured."

Tommy sat at the head of the table nearest to the door.

"Chief Jager," JJ said. "Can we summarize what we know?"

"Mr. Rodreguiz, I got the statements from all the Rangers before they left, so we can skip that portion. Please, share your perspective on the interlocking events in this unfathomable assault on humans that occurred in Magnolia Bluff."

"When Jo and I arrived for our holiday, Flower was in the middle of launching a podcast hosted by the Crimson Hat ladies. We discovered threats to the ladies and at every venue planned over several days. Jo spotted Camila for an instant in the crowd, and it haunted her. We were sucked in because something felt wrong." He continued with his point of view until he assembled a thorough flow of the case and various events. "Chief Jager, I apologize for not finding the evidence fast enough for Mateo to be arrested."

"That's not fair to act like it's your fault," Madison protested. "Because of you and Jo's dedication, we rescued kids who would have otherwise perished, bagged three bad guys, and halted a human trafficking operation in our backyard. Quite an accomplishment."

"Chief, this is my fault," Gloria volunteered. "I should have…" She got choked up. "Here's my badge, my weapon, and my keys to the cruiser."

Madison patted her arm and smiled.

Tommy's phone played *Send in the Clowns*. "Hang on, y'all." He answered the call. "Afternoon, Sam. How much pecan whiskey do I owe you?" Tommy's face went ashen. He flipped the phone to speaker and set the device on the table. "Sam, I have you on speaker. We have a mixed group listening."

"That was quite a lead you gave us here in Laredo. Thanks for alerting us. None of my people got hit. I can't say the same for the Coyotes operating the immigrant smuggling to this area. A fair-sized inventory was intercepted. That elderly couple you asked about were indeed hostages. They'd taken some hits and endured rough conditions. We've got them over at the hospital for medical attention."

Gloria cried out and clung to Madison sobbing.

"Sorry, I've got more. We nosed around the property. Sadly, we found a couple of unmarked graves. Whoever this bunch is that operated on this ranch, had no concept of decency when burying the bodies. Coroner will need to provide the details after his autopsy."

"I'm glad you were able to get there and that the lead was solid. I'll need your report to go along with mine. I'll get the whiskey packed up tomorrow. If you can email the report and overnight a hardcopy, I'd appreciate it."

"Sounds good. I'll ship it tonight. Today was my kind of day. A bad one for the crooks. Thank your undercover resource for me."

Tommy punched the end call button and barked, "Deputy Mendoza, you're out of uniform. Put that badge on and cinch up that weapon. There are civilians in the room."

He turned to the others in the room. "Gloria was undercover on this operation. JJ and Jo added a special perspective that is appreciated by myself and the entire town, if I know my gossipy podcasters. Madison, I appreciate your willingness to help with this case and step in as a deputy for me. All information related to this case is classified due to the federal laws broken. Our documentation is destined for the feds. I will need to capture the details of your involvement, and this office will interview those connected to the podcasts."

Gloria's crying was subsiding. Madison consoled her and whispered, "It's going to be alright, Gloria. We believed in you."

CHAPTER THIRTY-EIGHT

New Beginnings

Jo placed a reassuring hand on Ann's shoulder. Hank and Ann huddled with Camila and Renata. Jo stood and moved in front of the four like a barrier. She cleared her throat and looked Tommy straight in the eye, searching for his heart. "Chief Jager, please don't send these girls to an uncaring agency."

Ann and Hank dabbed with a tissue to catch their tears while both girls stoically looked at their hands.

"I said we'd discuss it, and it only makes sense to—"

"We're going to adopt them, Chief," Hank announced. "We want Camila and Renata in our family."

Ann grabbed his hand and nodded. "We've tried for kids of our own. This looks like our prayers have been answered. We've done our homework on adoption and spoken to our lawyer. The only question is if the girls will have us."

Jo translated what was being asked. Sniffling, the girls threw their arms around Hank and Ann. "*Si, si!*"

"I've spoken with the girls several times," Jo added. "They don't have anyone to return to. Their aunt sold them after their parents died. The buyers brought them to America, while the girls believed they'd get a chance at the American dream. They had no idea how awful the conditions would be: caged like animals and threatened into obedience. Chief, I'd like to take the girls to your office with JJ for a few minutes."

He nodded assent.

Jo closed the door and spoke only in Spanish. "Girls, JJ and I have discussed this. You need to have those computer chips removed as soon as possible. They link you to a place you don't ever want to go."

JJ turned on his app and showed the tracking. "Removing the chips will prevent these evil men from finding you. You're no one's property. Ever."

Jo discreetly showed them her scar. "The doctor won't leave a large scar like I have. When they are out, you won't be grabbed by anyone from your past. But you will likely have to speak with more law enforcement, perhaps from federal agencies. Hank and Ann will sign papers to sponsor you. They've spoken to their attorney."

Both nodded and their eyes filled with tears.

"We'll do this together at the doctor," Renata responded.

They returned to the conference room. Camila saw Gloria outside and stopped in front of her. In Spanish she confessed, "Miss Jo told me you wanted the donut thief. I tell you, it's me. As the oldest female I went to town with the one JJ called Nacho to get girl stuff. I was hungry. We all were. I asked for donuts. Nacho snarled; said no. He laughed. He wouldn't buy us food, but he'd wait while I stole it. I learned to be quick. I stole that man's box of donuts and pushed them out the back door. Then I left out the front and ran around to the back and grabbed them. I was ashamed to steal, but so hungry. Nacho took one. I smuggled the others to our pit. I wanted to eat them all. The other children's faces said they were starving, but their voices said nothing. Everybody got one. A few days later Nacho took me out. I stole another box. I got back and shared. Two were left over. We split them. The next week four were left. We each had one. I was hurting to get more to eat." Then in English she added, "I'm sorry."

Gloria sobbed and her shoulders shook.

"Camila," Jo suggested, "it would show you to be a good person if you offered to work off the debt for stealing the donuts."

Wiping her tears, Gloria objected. "Nooooooo. I'll pay for the donuts! I owe her that much and more."

"Gloria, we can discuss it later," suggested Tommy. "I think it best you go down to Laredo to take care of your folks. I'll expect you back in a couple of weeks after you're sure they can resume ranch work. You have your job, but family comes first."

Gloria nodded. "Thank you, Chief."

Tommy, thoroughly tired of the day and the drama, stopped in the restroom and washed his face before swallowing crow. He grabbed his cell and placed a call. "Hi, Lily, it's Tommy. I need to feed a sentimental bunch of people tonight. I knew you'd be the best place in town. Can you handle ten or so of us? I know you were assaulted..."

Tommy felt stunned at her response. "Does your mother know you use words like that, young lady?...We cracked our case wide open. I think that JJ and Jo are leaving in the morning. I hoped we'd celebrate; I'll bring some pecan whiskey...Thanks, Lily. We'll be there around seven."

CHAPTER THIRTY-NINE

Future Plans

Jo heard Lily in the kitchen echoing into the entry as she and JJ arrived. She looked at JJ and smiled as she led them toward the doorway.

"Lily, it's Jo. JJ is with me. Please don't shoot. We've had enough violence for one day."

"Come on in," Lily replied. "I heard some of it from Tommy. Glad you two weren't caught in the crossfire. Gossip is running wild with lots of noise about who did what. I look forward to seeing everyone together to hear the real scoop."

Jo noticed Lily's slowed movements and grimace lines across her face when she reached down for a bowl. "Lily, you're moving a little show. How are you feeling?"

"I'll be right as rain in a few days. I'm planning my moves for greater efficiency. It's not about quantity, but quality, right? Dinner will be ready soon."

"What's for supper, Lily? Jo and I talked about your food nonstop on the drive back," JJ said.

Jo had heard his stomach growl on their return trip. "He's hungry, Lily."

"Good. Tonight's TexMex night. I've got a couple of dishes of enchiladas in the oven—beef and chicken, of course. I'm working on the vegetables to go with chicken fajitas. Then my special homemade guacamole. I've several jars of my picante ready to use as needed. I think you two will like the spice and slight punch these have. Then I need to work on the black beans and refried. Easy, peasy and crowd pleasing round here."

"Sounds to me like we should address you as Master Chef Lily." Jo bowed as if addressing royalty.

Lily laughed. "I've wanted to be addressed as *The Chosen One According to the Prophecy* since I was little. Would that work instead?"

"Sounds wonderful, *Oh Chosen One*." JJ leaned over and kissed Jo on the cheek. "I'm heading upstairs. I'll check in the office and confirm our revised flight times."

Jo hugged JJ. "I'll be up in a little bit. I want to visit with Lily before everyone arrives." She sighed as he left.

"Jo, honey, you don't have to stick around. I'm not moving fast, but I can still get this done. Bruised and stiff with a lingering dose of mad is all."

"I wanted to speak with you in private."

"Sounds intriguing. What can I do for you?"

"Lily, it seems Renata and Camila want to live with Hank and Ann. They're planning to adopt them."

"That's a good thing. Ann's wanted a child for years, so a couple of troubled teens may answer her calling to motherhood."

"Yes, she said as much a while ago. Camila is all about the ranch and livestock. She's in love with horses, which I can't blame her. Hank has some great ones. She's not afraid of hard work either, so it should work out."

Lily moved on to mashing up the ingredients for green creamy chip dip. "So how does that involve me? I haven't ridden in years."

Jo chuckled. "There I go, back through the bakery, like JJ chides me. It only happens when I'm comfortable with someone."

She cleared her throat. "It's Renata. She's not much of an animal person. She's trying to learn English and wants to go to school if she can. Cooking is a passion of hers. When she was young, and her mama was alive, she helped cook. Her papa gave her to her aunt after her mama died so he could grieve in a bottle. Her aunt sold her. People in Magnolia Bluff brag about your cooking. Renata's overheard the tales and would like to learn cooking from you. She mentioned her specialty was breakfast burritos which sounds like a complement to what you're planning for tonight."

Lily considered while chopping up a storm. "Jo, I don't like anyone in my kitchen, outside of talking with someone, like we are on occasion. However, don't repeat this, I'm moving slowly and hurting from that attack. Having some help is a good idea. I think I could get used to her. I enjoyed her company when we had our evening together."

"I could get someone to drop her off if you want some help tonight. You could use it as a breaking in period, test her out. It could make your evening easier."

"That's a great idea. Can you call?"

Jo nodded and took out her cell.

Lily chuckled as her own phone rang. She looked at the screen. "Ah, I need to take this call from my podcasting pontificators. I bet they heard your news."

She turned away. "Hey, Mary Lou…I'm glad y'all can make it. I'll put a sign up for a private party, no problem." Frowning, Lily took a deep breath. "No, I heard Mateo got away…" She nodded. "If you bring some pecan or French vanilla ice cream to go with the pecan whiskey that would be perfect."

Jo placed her call. "Hi, Madison. Would you mind bringing Renata over to help Lily prepare for tonight?…No, not everyone until seven…Perfect, I'll let her know."

Jo disconnected. "Madison will drop her off in ten. Once she arrives, I think I'll go up and change. I might lay down for a few minutes."

"Jo, you do look a little tired. Grab a bottle of water from the fridge and sit until she arrives."

Jo opened the bottle. Suddenly her phone played *Wind Beneath My Wings*. She grinned. "I need to step outside for a minute and take this, Lily. Be right back."

Jo walked out the service door into the dining room. "Hi, Lara. How are you?...JJ said he phoned you, and all was well since the shoot was delayed...Oh good, I'm glad you're not mad...Yes, we're having a different sort of getaway, for sure...

She bent to deadhead a petunia, the phone slipping a bit from her ear. "Our flights are tomorrow evening...I'll fill you in... No, the food is good, but I haven't gained a pound. Everything should fit perfect...I love you too. See you soon."

Jo turned and spotted a wide-eyed Lily in the doorway. "Hi, Lily, do you need something?"

"I think I just got confirmation of something that's been kicking around in my mind since I met you. Your photo is on the cover of last month's *World Celebs* magazine. You wore makeup and clothes while here, just like any pretty girl, but you're JoW, the top young model from Brazil, right?"

"I hoped no one would recognize me. Please don't share with your friends."

"Oh, honey, I'd never say anything. We're friends. I'd like an autograph before you check out tomorrow, though, right on that cover. No one in town reads that magazine; they love those gossip rags better."

Jo hugged Lily. "I'm happy to give you that. I don't take friends lightly. I think our futures are bright."

CHAPTER FORTY

It's Party Time

Renata arrived full of energy and a contagious smile. "Miss Lily, thank you for giving me a chance," she said slowly in broken English.

Lily laughed. In broken Spanish she conveyed, "We'll figure it out and teach each other our languages. I don't know if you can read Spanish, but I translated my secret recipes onto my tablet for you. I'd like you to get the ingredients for each and set them in a spot."

Renata nodded and looked at the first recipe. "Got it." She quickly located the items and stacked them for staging, then went to the next.

"That's it, Renata. You've got this. Jo, you can leave us be. We need room to work, and you have your chores."

Jo smiled and laughed as she left. "See you at quarter to seven. Text if you need anything."

The laughter and chatter echoed as she went up the stairs.

JJ left their room around six-thirty that evening to see if he might lend a hand. The scent of fresh flowers, spicy Mexican delights, candles, and country music filled the dining room.

"Lily, Renata...this looks so inviting."

Renata poked her head up back in the corner where she completed setting the last table and replied in Spanish, "Señor JJ, you are early. I am almost done, but I could use a little help, please."

"Certainly. Whatcha need?"

"Lily wanted the Private Party Sign on the window, but I don't know how to do that. I found a hammer and nail but didn't want to hit the glass."

"Good call," JJ admitted with a small chuckle. "I think she has tape at the check-in desk." He rummaged around. "Yep, here you go."

Renata looked at it. "I don't know what this is, sir. Show me, please."

"This is clear tape and is sticky on one side." He pulled off a strip and attached it to her thumb. "Tear off two more pieces and attach to the top and bottom of the sign. I'll hold it for you."

She stuck out the tip of her tongue while concentrating. "I see." She put the sign into position and pressed it firm to the window. "Lily will be happy. I finished everything she asked."

JJ liked that the young teen looked pleased. "Renata, Lily would have told you if you didn't understand. Don't be afraid to ask her questions if something's unfamiliar."

Lily pressed through the service door carrying a chafing dish for the sideboard. "JJ, you don't need to worry about that. This sweetie asks questions about everything. The best part is, she remembers the answers. I am so glad she's here."

Renata rushed over, gently taking the container. "I put this one on the second holder and light the heater underneath."

"You got it, sweetie. JJ, come help carry a few more of the serving dishes out, please."

"Yes, ma'am."

Minutes later everything was positioned. Lily went to make certain the elements in the kitchen were shut off and returned without her apron, fluffing her hair. "Renata, go wash your hands in the same bedroom you slept in when you were here, and change your shirt. I want you with me to greet our guests."

Renata dashed up the stairs.

"JJ, you wouldn't like to play bartender until Tommy gets here, would you?"

"Of course. What's your pleasure?"

"I'd like a glass of red wine. Fix something for yourself and Jo while you're at it. She's headed down."

"Jo, honey, what would you like, wine or to wait for the pecan whiskey?"

"I'd like some white wine, please," Jo affirmed as she walked in the dining room. "It's beautiful. What a fast transformation."

"Thanks to the extra pair of hands, it was a snap."

They sat at the front table and clicked glasses just as Renata noiselessly slipped in.

"Lily, you're an amazing proprietor. Thank you for an interesting vacation," JJ toasted.

"We aim to please, but this trip for you two was nowhere in my crystal ball."

The door opened and guests piled in. Daphne and Caroline stepped into the room with LouEllen and Valerie right behind. Hugs were exchanged between all the podcasters.

"Girls, you need to meet Renata. She helped with tonight's meal, and hopefully after I speak to Hank and Ann, I can have her part time during school and full time on breaks."

Renata beamed, politely shaking hands with each lady in turn, followed by a "Nice to meet you."

Hank, Ann, and Camila walked in with Tommy and Madison hot on their heels.

While everyone greeted, Tommy announced, "I brought the star beverage and now the bar is open. I'll serve."

Everyone laughed and dutifully stepped into place with their drink orders, which Tommy filled with precision.

"This is totally self-serve tonight. Sit wherever you like. We're all friends," Lily stated.

Folks filled plates and found chairs. Discussions of the recent events made the rounds, with clarity inserted on specific points as needed.

"Ladies," Tommy said, "I am sorry I didn't put enough emphasis on your complaints. While Gloria is with her folks in Laredo, Madison will fill in and be happy to deliver your complaints."

Madison deadpanned, "Thanks, Chief."

JJ, sharing a plate of food with Jo, enjoyed the comradery of the group. "These are nice folks. Are you glad we came here, Jo, or wished I'd picked something like glamping?"

"JJ, glamping looked like fun: remote and quiet. If we'd done that, I'd never have honed my detective skills. Speaking of which, I wonder why the head of our podcasters is late. It's nearly eight and I took her as totally punctual."

"You're right." He looked around. "Caroline or Valerie, any idea where Mary Lou is? I figured she'd want one more show tonight with everyone assembled."

Caroline and Valerie looked anxious. All the podcasters checked their phones and frowned.

The front door swung open with a clunk as the handle hit the wall. A disheveled, teary Mary Lou entered wheeling her chair with her laptop braced in her legs. "JJ, are you around? I need you!" she shrieked.

"I'm coming."

She picked up the laptop and shoved the laptop into his hands. Mary Lou's hands shook, and tears streamed down her face.

JJ held the laptop in one hand and escorted her to a table. "Tommy, I think we need a shot of your famous whiskey over here. Ladies, while I look at the issue, allow Mary Lou to catch her breath. Don't crowd her."

Tommy brought the drink and a box of tissues, setting them down beside her. "Yell if you need anything, JJ."

The image that appeared on the screen of her PC showed Mary Lou with no legs and most of her hair pulled out, tears streaming down her face. Pure threat tactic. JJ took a photo with his cell phone. "Jo, please go grab my laptop bag and all, honey."

Jo returned and caught sight of the screen. "Oh, my gosh. Mary Lou, can I get you another drink?"

JJ powered up his spare machine and attached it to her laptop. His fingertips flew across the keys as he copied various files. While working, he questioned Mary Lou. "Do you recall how this started?"

"I turned on my laptop and to schedule a meeting that I could launch later, thinking we could do a final show. I knew everyone would be here. I established the links between my laptop and my cloud storage." She threw back the first drink as Jo set the second one down. "I thought I'd better check the podcast website to see how many hits we had, and found some comments needing a reply. There were a slew of known names which have followed us closely, plus several new first-time viewers."

"That makes perfect sense. Then what?"

"When I responded to the last comment, a new name showed up with a medal image, like a first-place badge. I figured we'd been shared enough to hit a high view number and we were getting an achievement award. Then I noticed it was time to leave for this party. I couldn't help it. I wanted to see it before I shared so

I clicked the link. My entire machine started making noise like bombs going off. Loud whistling and bright explosions like you get in war movies. Then this thing entered the screen and filled it with a creepy screechy laugh. You know, psychotic like. My hands shook so bad I couldn't turn it off."

"Good thing you didn't. Makes it easier for me. Then what?"

"Then I got this text message." Mary Lou handed him her phone.

Now you've got nothing, la puta.

"The files on my laptop vanished like coins being consumed by Super Mario, which I'm sure you know nothing about."

"I totally understand," he chuckled. "Go on."

"That's it. Then this monster distortion appeared. I knew I had to bring it to you." Fresh tears streaked her cheeks, and all the ladies of her group encircled her with murmurs. "Everything's gone. I'm so sorry. This is my ego, and it's ugly."

"You go sit with the ladies. Hey, Tommy, can you come here, please?"

"What's up?"

"I'm not certain why she knew not to shut it down. Do you have a number to call that fed agent assigned to your case? I think we can target the location of the cyber-attacks. They have no way of knowing we know anything."

"Okay, I'll call. Let's move over to the sitting room."

"Hey all, eat and drink. We've got this. Mary Lou, you are one brave lady. It'll be alright."

Special Agent Welch arrived thirty minutes later. He listened intently to the particulars and took the machine with the files earmarked by JJ. He promised to update Tommy the next day, indicating he was confident an arrest or two could be made. Tommy went along to also turn over the prisoners to Welch's team for further questioning.

JJ returned to the party in the dining room. Everyone looked at him. He smiled. "The good news is Mary Lou saved the day by not turning off her machine. I recovered quite a bit of information that will allow the feds to trace the threat to its source. I suspected before that Mateo hired a contractor to do threats to warn you off. Mateo is on a Top Ten wanted list with his picture at every entry point. I don't think he's in this country, but safe in his home in Mexico." JJ frowned and noticed the disappointment on their faces. "Annoying, I know, but he won't show his face here again."

Then JJ grinned. "Tommy arranged for federal agents to remain in town for a couple of months. They'll come introduce themselves. They're here to keep an eye on things."

Cheers erupted. Jo rushed up to be enclosed in JJ's arms. "JJ, I'm bushed."

"Me, too. Folks, we need to call it a night. We've got to leave after breakfast in the morning to make our plane. Lily, can I get another bottle of that wonderful bubbly to take up with us?"

"You sure can. Renata, would you please grab the one in the fridge and take it up along with the chocolate strawberries we made earlier."

"*Si*, Miss Lily."

They turned and headed up to their room. They took a leisurely bath in the enormous tub, and then snuggled into bed. JJ turned out the light. Jo whispered, "I think we need to return next year."

They both giggled and drifted off to sleep.

The Magnolia Bluff Crime Chronicles
continues with *The Shine from a Girl in the Lake*,
by Richard Schwindt, coming to a bookseller near you.
Enjoy an excerpt right now!

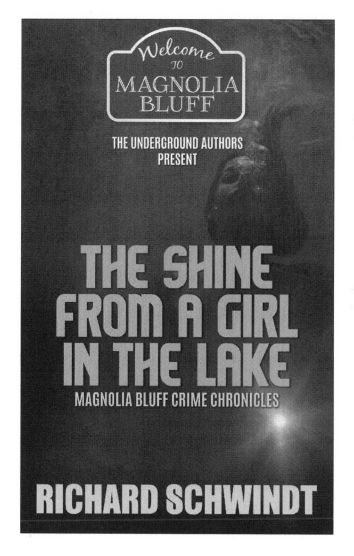

CHAPTER FOUR

Tuesday Morning

My ten o'clock class on the psychology of personality was about to begin when I arrived at the college. My head felt soft; a massive ache lurked in the shadows, waiting for one wrong move to set it free.

Some of the kids in the class would be the same ones I lectured on binge drinking yesterday. Hell.

I don't know what time I got to O'Gara's bar, at the other end of Magnolia Bluff, but I have a vague memory of watching baseball on a television over the bar, downing Lone Stars and shots.

By the end of the night, little memory had imprinted; maybe a vague recollection of a blonde dude standing up and saying he was officer Dinky, Winky, or something. He requested my truck keys, then asked one of his buddies to drive me to my house.

I blacked out, again. Now I had to take a cab, and figure out what he had done with my keys.

Undergraduates, not always the brightest of God's creatures, know a hangover when they see one.

"What were you up to last night, Professor Kurelek?"

"Did you notice any cognitive impairment?"

"Does it really effect the central nervous system?

As I braced for ninety minutes of academic purgatory, a knock sounded from the door, and Valerie stuck in her head. She wore a smug expression that told me nothing good.

"Professor Jafari would like to see you Dr. Kurelek."

"Right now?"

"Yes, she said to dismiss your class."

I turned back to the room. "Read Chapter 12 through 16 for Thursday. See you then." They were whispering to each other, even as they left.

I think Valerie wanted me to follow her, but I strode ahead not wanting to be her water carrier. What on earth did Shadia want enough to make me cancel my class? God, I hope no one saw me and complained last night. Did I do something stupid?

Once in the office, I could tell right away that Shadia was upset. No banter or inane, or insightful remarks. Just her sitting very still behind the desk, eyes searching mine. Princess was nowhere in sight, probably banished to the garden.

She was not alone. A bespectacled man, fiftyish, in an old suit, stood beside her.

I came close to saying "Who died?" but my therapist skills saved me at the last minute. Best to be tentative; let someone tell me what was going on. It took a moment, but the man finally spoke.

"Dr. Kurelek?"

"Yes. And you are?"

He stepped forward and extended a hand. "I'm an investigator with the police. My name is Reece Sovern."

I shook his hand, and asked the obvious question. "What brings you here?" I looked down at Shadia, who glanced away. "Why is my class canceled?"

"You don't know?"

"No idea. Has something happened?"

He glanced down at his notepad. Then cleared his throat. "This morning, at approximately 7 am, Judge Peacock decided to cast for bass from the dock by his bait shop on the reservoir." He looked up at me for some reason. I was listening.

"After taking a few casts, he was briefly blinded by a sudden glint below the dock. Looking again to that spot, he saw what appeared to be a mass in the water. On closer scrutiny, he saw it was a body in the lake. Putting down his fishing rod, he jumped off the dock and dragged the body to shore, determined that it was deceased, and called the police."

"My God, that's awful. Is he okay? Does he want to see me?"

Shadia glanced away again. Then looked back at me. "Michael. You need to keep listening to Mr. Sovern."

On cue, he spoke: "Dr. Kurelek. Can you describe your movements last night and this morning?"

My adrenal system jumped into action. This was out of a television mystery, but I was present, with two sets of eyes boring a hole in mine. I detected a quaver in Shadia, but the detective was cold as ice.

I took a breath. "I think I need to know what is going on."

"Can you start by telling me your movements?"

All kinds of emotions were triggered now; I had to stay calm and willed myself to do so. I had been investigated before. "Okay, fine. I did sessions here at the college until just after nine, then drove across town to O'Gara's for drinks."

"And after that?"

"I'm not sure."

"Why not?"

"I was too drunk. Someone may have driven me home."

Shadia looked wounded, wondering why her clinical psychologist was blackout drunk on a Monday night.

"You don't really know exactly what you did last night, do you?" He didn't wait for an answer. "Do you know a Marianne Blye?"

I was immediately struck by a wave of nausea. I glanced for a chair, found one, and sat, saying nothing. I didn't know what to say. Therapists don't just blurt out their patient's name.

The cat jumped on my lap. I guess she was still in here after all. I choked down a sob. The saddest indicator of alcohol poisoning has to be pathos of remorse and tears waiting to escape. I thought about Marianne.

"We know from your datebook that you saw Ms. Blye last night."

"Valerie gave you my datebook! That's confidential." I felt stupid as soon as the words emerged. Violation of patient confidentiality is a disaster for therapists, but this was worse. "Marianne wasn't suicidal when she left. She denied any thoughts of self-harm, and she had disclosed something personal and important. I agreed to see her later this week. I thought she wanted to talk more."

"When was that supposed to be?"

"Thursday at eight. It's in the datebook too."

"I saw that."

Then why the hell did you ask?

"Another evening session."

"It was all I had available." The cat had settled in my lap and, failing to read the room, started to purr. I found myself unconsciously stroking its fur.

"You're saying it might be something other than suicide, Dr. Kurelek."

I looked up sharply. "I don't know what happened. You mean it isn't suicide?"

He paused and looked through his spectacles at me. Then he turned towards Shadia, as if he needed her permission, and said, "He needs to come to the station." He then turned back to me: "I have more questions to ask. I am going to need to know about that personal matter she discussed with you."

Shadia found her voice. "Go Michael. I think it may be prudent for Valerie to cancel your appointments for the rest of the day."

"Her parents... Marianne's parents live in Seattle."

"Mr. Sovern has all the information. Take care of yourself, Michael." Shadia kept her voice neutral but I could imagine the disappointment she felt in me. This would be all over the college before I reached his car.

"You don't have to, you know, ah, put handcuffs on me, do you?"

He smiled; the first sign of any human warmth. "You are not under arrest. We just want your help right now. You have the right to refuse to come with me."

The cat was happy, but it was time to give her back to Shadia. "It's okay. If I can help, I will."

I was conscious of how far and how quickly I had regressed to an almost infantile sense of vulnerability and need. Time to pull myself together. There would be a few minutes in the car to put myself in a self-hypnotic trance, and place some suggestions for calm and composure.

He didn't handcuff me, but led me into the back seat of his Ford. I saw the blue expanse of Burnet Reservoir as we pulled out of the College drive and turned towards Magnolia Bluff proper.

Normally, I loved the lake, fishing for bass, swimming out to the center and back. Now, today, the water looked cold, oily, and lonely, having this morning disgorged one of its dead.

A clutch of sycamores by the lake bent in a protracted gust of wind.

I thought about Judge Peacock. It seemed ridiculous to me that a Judge ran a bait and tackle shop, more so that he appeared to love it so much. Made me wonder what he thought about making his living as a judge. Maybe I was about to find out.

I'm sure he would have strong feelings towards whoever made him stagger from the water bearing the corpse of a young woman. He wasn't a young man. It must have been hellishly difficult.

Mostly I thought about poor Marianne sipping primly from her coffee cup in my office, dying alone, in a strange place, away from home.

The painful disclosure about her father's affair was made for nothing at all; now about to be repeated to a detective.

Time to lay back in the seat and start the self-hypnosis.

ABOUT THE **MAGNOLIA BLUFF CRIME CHONICLES**

What is a multi-author crime novel series is the question CW Hawes got when he proposed the idea to our fellow Underground Authors.

We'd just collaborated on a short story anthology, and CW was interested in taking the idea of collaboration to the next level. A multi-author series is what happens when a group of authors decides to write a series of novels. In the case of the Magnolia Bluff Crime Chronicles, the Underground Authors decided to create a fictional town that would be the common denominator for each of the books throughout the series.

Each author would have his or her characters, perhaps use some of the characters the other authors created, but the action would take place in the beautiful little Texas Hill Country town of Magnolia Bluff. Nine authors showing us nine different sides of the town. We'll experience humor, dark dilemmas, suspense, romance, thrills and spills—all told through a whole lot of good storytelling. The kind that will keep you up past your bedtime, or make you miss your bus stop. Stay tuned. There's lots happening in Magnolia Bluff. And you don't want to miss any of it. We're even considering a season two.

MAGNOLIA BLUFF CRIME CHONICLES

About the Authors

Breakfield – Works for a high-tech manufacturer as a solution architect, functioning in hybrid data/telecom environments. He considers himself a long-time technology geek, who also enjoys writing, studying World War II history, travel, and cultural exchanges. Charles' love of wine tastings, cooking, and Harley riding has found ways into the stories. As a child, he moved often because of his father's military career, which even helps him with the various character perspectives he helps bring to life in the series. He continues to try to teach Burkey humor.

Burkey – Works as a business architect who builds solutions for customers on a good technology foundation. She has written many technology papers, white papers, but finds the freedom of writing fiction a lot more fun. As a child, she helped to lead the kids with exciting new adventures built on make believe characters, was a Girl Scout until high school, and contributed to the community as a young member of a Head Start program. Rox enjoys family, learning, listening to people, travel, outdoor activities, sewing, cooking, and thinking about how to diversify the series.

Breakfield and Burkey – started writing non-fictional papers and books, but it wasn't nearly as fun as writing fictional stories. They found it interesting to use the aspects of technology that people are incorporating into their daily lives more and more as a perfect way to create a good guy/bad guy story with elements of travel to the various places they have visited either professionally and personally, humor, romance, intrigue, suspense, and a spirited way to remember people who have crossed paths with them. They love to talk about their stories with private and public book readings. Burkey also conducts regular interviews for Texas authors, which she finds very interesting. Her first interview was, wait for it, Breakfield. You can often find them at local book fairs or other family-oriented events.

The primary series is based on a family organization called R-Group. Recently they have spawned a subgroup that contains some of the original characters as the Cyber Assassins Technology Services (CATS) team. The authors have ideas for continuing the series in both of these tracks. They track the more than 150 characters on a spreadsheet, with a hidden avenue for the future coined The Enigma Chronicles tagged in some portions of the stories. Fan reviews seem to frequently suggest that these would make good television or movie stories, so the possibilities appear endless, just like their ideas for new stories.

They have book video trailers for each of the stories, which can be viewed on YouTube, Amazon's Authors page, or on their website, *www.EnigmaBookSeries.com*. Their website is routinely updated with new interviews, answers to readers' questions, book trailers, and contests. You may also find it fascinating to check out the fun acronyms they create for the stories summarized on their website. Reach out to them at *Authors@EnigmaSeries.com, Twitter@EnigmaSeries,* or *Facebook@TheEnigmaSeries.*

Please provide a fair and honest review on amazon
and any other places you post reviews. We appreciate the feedback.

Other stories by Breakfield and Burkey in
The Enigma Series are at **www.EnigmaBookSeries.com**

We would greatly appreciate
if you would take a few minutes
and provide a review of this work
on Amazon, Goodreads
and any of your other favorite places.

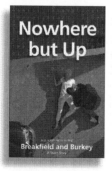

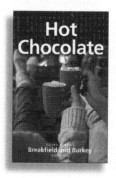

12405648R00113